CONVICTIONS *of* FAMILY

WRITTEN BY:
CHRISTOPHER "TOON" WILLIAMS

...I give my deepest appreciation
for those who have shown
themselves to be family. Don't
fail to do the same.

Sincerely,
Joon
Romans 8:31

CONTENTS

PREFACE

First of all, I'm honored that you (or anyone for that matter) would take the time to purchase (hopefully) and open a book with my name on the cover. Why? Well, for the majority of my life, though a leader in many circles, I had very little to say that was worthy of your attention. Honest self-reflection has not been kind to my ego. However, it has been helpful in ways I never would've imagined.

Anyway, since you have chosen to read up to this point, let me be clear concerning the contents of this book. I don't want anyone to feel cheated. I've experienced that before. I didn't like it. I figure I'm not alone.

So, as you may have concluded based on the cover, this novel has three main focuses: family, faith, and the causes and effects of incarceration. I am a committed follower of the Lord Jesus Christ, but this is not a "Christian novel," per se. It is a novel written by a Christian. I'm from the hood and I've stomped in many of them, but this is not a "hood novel." It's about life, one I am very familiar with.

Due to some ridiculously foolish, hurtful, and selfish decisions, I have spent roughly two-thirds of my forty-six years on earth incarcerated. Group homes, juvenile facilities, jails, prisons—been there, done that.... sadly. In fact, I'm about to begin my twenty-fourth consecutive calendar year in prison as this novel goes into publication. So, I'm somewhat of an expert as it pertains to the aforementioned causes and effects of incarceration... again, sadly.

Why write this book? What makes it relevant? Well, for years there has been a fascination with prison life in movies, TV shows, documentaries, etc. There have been countless books written on the subject. Non-fiction, fiction, memoirs, you name it. I've read several of them over the years. However, for the most part, I've discovered that these representations are biased. They are so concentrated on gangs, violence, drugs, sex, and other illicit activities that they neglect to capture the humanity that exists in the midst of the inhumane.

In this book, there are moments of darkness. It would not be based in reality if it were not so. Yet, instead of prevailing darkness, light breaks forth through the clouds. Though fiction, this has been my prison experience for the past sixteen years. I just needed to have my eyes opened so I could see it... and be it for others.

CHAPTER 1

1996

The sudden knock on the door appeared to irritate Boss' mother as she was trying to focus on the questions being asked during the "Fast Money" segment on *Family Feud.*

"A blank check!" She answered quickly before yelling, "Who is it?"

"It's Crystal, Mama G!"

"Washing powder!" she shouted at the television. "Hold on girl!" Boss' mother called for his nephew to come open the door.

"Ma'am?" The voice of a preoccupied young boy hollered from the back of the house.

"I said, 'Come open this door, boy!'"

"Okay! Here I come!"

Seconds later a boy no older than ten came running out of the back room dressed in dingy Spiderman pajamas. Reaching the front door, he turned the porch light on and peeped through the screen door before unlocking it.

"What's up, Crystal?" he said, smiling until he noticed a man standing off to the side. "Who is that?"

"Boy, open the door. This is my friend."

"I thought you was Otis' girl? What you doing with him?" he asked, aiming a boyish scowl in her friend's direction.

"I am Otis' girl! My friend was nice enough to give me a ride over here and I wasn't about to let him sit in the car. Now, if you done with yo interrogation, open the door."

"Boy, if you don't open that door, you better!" Boss' mother screamed.

"Yeah boy, you better." Crystal teased.

Upon his grandmother's command, Boss' nephew relented and opened the door. Crystal stepped in, playfully slapping him on the back of the head. Her friend followed closely behind her. Now that his nephew could clearly see her face, he thought she looked nervous. But he was only ten. What did he know?

She walked into the living room and sat on the couch next to Boss' mother. Crystal's friend stood, leaning on a chair close to the door trying not to be suspicious. Crystal tried to make small talk with Ms. G, who now appeared to be engrossed in a Coca Cola commercial.

"So how have you been, Mama G?"

"Oh, I'm good baby," she replied, eyes still locked on the television.

"Do you need anything?"

"Nah baby, I'm fine. God is still good. He's keeping the electricity on and a lil food in the kitchen. That's enough for me."

"Amen, Mama G," Crystal responded, with a lot less certainty. "Where's sis? At work?"

"Yeah, I don't really like her working at night like this, but she gotta do what she gotta do, I guess."

"I guess," Crystal said. "I wish Otis was here. I still can't believe ain't nobody heard from him. I hope he's all right."

Boss' mother took her eyes off the TV for the first time since they had come and carefully surveyed the room. She looked at Crystal, who appeared nervous. Her eyes were wide and a bit wild despite her efforts to conceal it. She turned to look at Crystal's friend. "How are you doing, young man?" she asked, ignoring Crystal's veiled dig for information.

"I'm okay, ma'am," he answered with a Hispanic accent.

"So how do you know Crystal?" she continued.

"Oh," he said, unnerved by the questions," I met her through Big O... I mean, through your son."

"So, you know my son?"

"Yes, ma'am."

"Okay. Good." She turned back to Crystal with knowing eyes and calmly stated, "No Crystal, Otis hasn't been in contact with us since he left. Whatever caused him to leave so urgently is his business. It doesn't concern anyone who lives here."

She paused as if to gather her thoughts. Everyone remained silent waiting for her to resume. She turned back toward Crystal's friend. "I hope and pray that what he had going on gets worked out one way or another. I don't expect to hear from him until then, and that's how I prefer it."

He just nodded his head. Crystal looked at him, then Boss' mother, hoping her answers were satisfactory. Sensing something in the atmosphere, Boss' nephew came and stood next to his grandmother. Crystal stood up and hugged them both. Then she and her friend left. Boss' nephew closed the door behind them, making sure it was locked.

When they got to the parking lot Crystal looked at her friend and said, "I told you she didn't know anything."

"Shut up and get in the car!" he growled through clenched teeth. As soon as the door shut, he reached over and back handed her in her face.

"What the ...?" Crystal cried out, tears welling up in her eyes. Before she could finish her sentence, he had a nine-millimeter pointed at her swollen stomach.

"Now listen to me," he said calmly, "you can get any ideas of us coming to an understanding out of your mind. Your dude put an end to that when he violated me and my home by taking what didn't belong to him. So, you better start taking this a bit more seriously, because I got pressure on me to account for what he took. And before I take this loss all by myself," he spewed venomously, tapping her stomach with the gun, "I'll kill that sweet, innocent old lady in there, his hardworking sister, his dingy little nephew, you, and his unborn child! You feeling me, feeling me, feeling me..."

Boss jerked out of his sleep, anxious and sweaty. Man! Another one of those dreaded nightmares. They seemed to get more vivid every time. Wiping tears away with the palms of his hands, an uneasy feeling settled over him. He naturally assumed it was due to the dream and dismissed it.

Getting out of bed, he stood up and stretched. Boss was a big man; 6'4", 245 pounds solid. His dark complexion and penetrating hazel brown eyes were a physical contradiction that seemed to define his personality. Because of his massive frame, upon the first encounter you would expect him to be a brute. And he could be. However, once he began to speak, you became aware of an intellect that often overshadowed his size.

As his eyes adjusted to the darkness of the bedroom, he looked down at the woman lying on the bed. That calmed his nerves a bit. If there was ever a woman who embodied what God intended for Eve to be, as far as he was concerned, it was Ebony, a loyal mate, a trusted confidant, and a caring advisor. And although her petite frame might fool you, she was up to any physical challenge that came her way. Ride or die!

Sensing that she was being observed, Ebony opened her eyes and smiled brightly. "Look at you, up early in the morning stalking," she yawned out.

Boss returned the smile and reached down to grab a pack of cigarettes off the nightstand. He lit one, passed it to her, and then lit one for himself, taking a long pull off of it. Recognizing that something must be bothering him by the lack of a response to the shot she took at him, she asked, "What's wrong, baby? Another bad dream?"

"Yeah," he said despondently. "I'm stuck with those."

Ebony didn't know what to say. They had been through this many times before. It was part of their existence.

Lying back on the bed, she posed seductively and said, "Well, come on over here and take your frustrations out on me."

"Sometimes I think that's all you want me for," he said, trying to look serious but unable to disguise the playfulness in his voice.

"I wasn't aware that you were good for anything else," she threw back at him.

"Yeah, whatever!" he responded, with a hint of male pride.

She replied, "That's what I'm talking about: Whatever!"

Walking over to the bed, Boss leaned down and kissed her on the neck. With Ebony in his arms, he allowed himself to relax and forget about his demons. At least for the moment.

After a hot shower and breakfast, Boss started to get dressed. Ebony, still lying in the bed, looked at the clock and asked, "Where are you going this early in the morning?"

"Early? It's almost nine o'clock,"

"Yeah, but it's Monday. You don't cut no hair on Monday."

"Okay. But why you sound so suspicious?"

"You know why— Never mind."

Boss shook his head and laughed. "Baby, come on? I got a child with the girl! I can't stop her from calling me. It could be important, but she already knows what it is. And so should you!"

"I know baby, but—"

"But what?" he asked, cutting her off.

"You know." She shamefully dropped her head.

He walked over and sat on the bed next to her. "Ebony Latrice."

When she lifted her head, he looked lovingly into her eyes. "Baby, I need you to understand something, once and for all. I'm not one of those dudes out there looking to smash every female who opens her legs for me. And I'm not trying to be responsible for raising no football team. I have a child. Unfortunately, it's not with you. But she, or some other woman, could give me a house full of children, and not even come close to being the woman you are. For real."

He wiped the tears off her cheek and continued. "You make me a better person. Or at least you try. You push me, to the point where you get on my nerves," he nudged her with his shoulder and smiled, "but you're it, boo. I ain't letting you get away. All right?"

"I love you, Otis." Ebony was smiling again.

"I love you too, baby. But don't be questioning me about where I'm going no more," he said humorously as he was walking out of the bedroom. "You ain't got me *that* whipped."

"Not yet!" She fired back, and then he was out of the front door. Neither of them had any idea he would never walk through that door again.

CHAPTER 2

2005

"Class dismissed," said the professor.

Earnest "Silence" Boyd slid his locs over his eyes, picked up his books, and mobbed out of the classroom. He was not your typical college student. In fact, nothing about him was typical. He was only 5'8" and 165 pounds soaking wet, but he had the confident demeanor of a giant that caused people to look up to him. He didn't talk much, choosing not to "waste words with words." Yet, he could end any conversation with a mere look from his piercing eyes. Although he was a high-ranking gang member, suspected of a couple of murders, at the age of twenty-one he valued his concept of God, family, and education more than money, sex, and drugs.

Walking across the parking lot to his dark blue '85 Seville, he noticed the stares of admiration from the females and the disguised looks of hatred from his male counterparts, but he chose to acknowledge neither. Cranking up the "G Ride" he put on some old-school Pac. With "Shed So Many Tears" beating out of the speakers, he set off to his next destination.

Pulling up in front of the junior high school, Silence spotted his little brother Jerome talking to a girl, waiting for him to arrive. That brought a rare smile to his face. He loved Jerome more than anything in the world. He wanted to spend more time with him, but so far, their mother and father, Bobby and Tonya, wouldn't allow it. That's how he referred to his parents. Their relationship had been so strained over the years that he barely thought of them as family.

Cutting his mack game short upon seeing his brother, Jerome ran to the car. "What's up, big bruh?!" he yelled, slamming the door shut.

"Calm down, Super Fly! That lil gal got you so excited you gon tear the handle clean off," Silence said, smiling. "You probably didn't even get her number."

"Yeah, right. I learned from the best."

"Aright then," he said throwing up his hands in surrender. "So how was everything today?" he asked, driving away from the school.

"It was cool. I got an A- on that history test. But I barely passed the algebra exam we worked on."

And he was barely looking at his big brother, waiting for his response to the news. Silence invested a lot of time and energy making sure Jerome's grades were up to par.

"What does 'barely' mean, lil bruh?" he asked, glancing over at the passenger seat.

"I passed, bruh," Jerome answered, a bit dejected, but hoping his adamant stance would prove to be grounds for a reprieve.

"Yeah, I heard you, lil bruh. But you said, 'barely' passed." Silence seemed to be enjoying this exchange. "What does that mean? C- or a D+?"

"Come on, big bruh. I passed!" Jerome responded again, grinning.

"Boy, stop playing with me!" Silence laughed and gave him a brotherly punch in the arm.

"Ouch!" exclaimed Jerome, rubbing his arm. "Man, you gave me a frog."

"I'ma give you a bull frog if you keep playing with me," he threatened, clinching his fist again.

"Alright, bruh!" Jerome said, raising his hands to protect himself from another blow. "I made a C-. But bruh, that test was harrrd!"

"That's why it's called a test, lil bruh. It challenges you. And I know you're better than a C-. So, this weekend we'll be studying Algebra."

"But bruh," he contended, with a pained expression on his face. "I thought we were going to the mall?"

"We were. Now we're going to Algebra 101."

"Man..."

"Man, nothing. Anyway, what did they say about you spending the weekend with me?"

"They still tripping!" he said sadly. "Daddy stays so drunk that I really don't even like talking to him. And when I do, I always get a negative response. Like it is my fault he lost his damn job."

"Bruh, what did I tell you about that? Don't let that stuff into your vocabulary. Most people cuss because they don't have the words to express themselves otherwise. You do."

"My bad, big bruh."

"Has he put his hands on you?" He asked this with a concerned and threatening tone in his voice.

"Nah, bruh. He raises his voice sometimes. But other than that, he's been cool with me." He turned his head toward the window, but it was obvious he wanted to say more.

"What's up, lil bruh?" Silence inquired.

Jerome turned to face his big brother with tears welling up in his eyes. "Mama, man..." he sighed, holding back the flood gates. "She been getting it, bruh."

It hurt Silence to see his little brother like this, but he never minced words when it came to them.

"Look bruh, I know you don't understand this, but she's been getting it from dude for so long that she has to like it. And if she likes it, there is nothing you can do about it. Trust me, I tried. I'll never make that mistake again. I'm only concerned about you."

"I'm good, bruh." But it was obvious that he wasn't.

They made the remainder of the trip in their own thoughts. Their parents were always a topic of contention between them. Actually, it was the only one. Jerome worshipped his big brother, but he couldn't understand why he said some of the things he did about their parents. They weren't perfect, but they were theirs.

Pulling up in front of their parents' home, Silence turned the radio down. "They won't let you stay overnight, but we'll still spend the weekend together. I'll pick you up early tomorrow. We'll clean up the Chevy and hit the park after we leave the mall." He said, smiling.

"Bet! I love you, big bruh!" Jerome exclaimed, leaning over to give his brother a hug.

"I love you too, little bruh."

After making sure Jerome had made it inside safely, he smashed off. He could have sworn that he saw their mom peeking out of the living room window, but why bother? She had made her choice, and he had made his. *Only God can judge me*, he found himself thinking as he made his way home.

✝

As he walked through the front door, he noticed that the ringer on his phone had been off the whole time. He had three missed calls: two from his partners and one from his side chick. Man, he hadn't heard from her since that incident with his baby's mama. But tonight, she was exactly what he needed.

After making a few calls, he hopped into the shower to knock off the dirt of the day. But even standing under the hot, soothing flow of the water, frustration began to set in. He just didn't get his parents. They knew beyond a shadow of a doubt that he would care for and protect his brother with his own life. But just to hurt him, they did everything they could to keep them apart. The only reason they allowed them to be together as much as they did is because they didn't want to be bothered with certain parental responsibilities themselves.

Stepping out of the shower, he heard his house phone ringing, which was unusual because not many people had the number. Hurrying into the bedroom, he answered, "Hello?" Nothing. But he heard arguing in the background. "Hello?!"

"Earnest?" It was Jerome. And he was crying.

"Rome! What's wrong, lil bruh?"

"After you dro-dropped me off da-da-daddy started tri-tripping. Talking about how I was gon be a no-good cri-criminal just like you. I tried to just walk a-away, like you said. But today he wouldn't let it go. He ste-stepped in my way, and when I tried to push past him, he gra-grabbed me from be-behind, and started cho-cho-choking me, and..."

"I'm on my way, bruh!" Silence was in a calm rage. He had warned him, and now he was going to deal with him.

He threw on some clothes, grabbed a strap, snatched his keys off the dresser, and was out of the door. He couldn't afford to get pulled over, so he forced himself to slow down. With time to think about it, he knew that he really didn't want to kill the dude. That would crush Jerome. But he wouldn't accept another hand being laid on his little brother. So, he decided he would just beat the hell out of him and take Jerome over to their grandmother's house for a while. Let them call the police. He had a good lawyer. And he doubted they would want to have to explain his father's abusive behaviors.

He was right down the street now. He put the gun in the glove compartment. He parked the car and walked toward the front of the door. Jerome was waiting on him. He gave him a hug, looked him over to make sure he was okay, and asked, "Where is he at?"

"Don't wo-worry about it, bruh. Let's just go."

"Nah, lil bruh. I need to holler at him first."

"Please...." Jerome tried to plead.

"Get some clothes and wait for me in the car," he barked out.

Jerome rushed off to his bedroom. Silence made his way to the kitchen where he could hear his father still cussing out threats. *Where is Tonya*, he wondered? Entering the kitchen, he saw his father sitting at the kitchen table drinking Kessler straight out of the bottle.

Seeing Silence come in, he yelled, "What the hell you doing in my house, killa? You ain't got no business here!"

"My little brother is my business," Silence responded before he rushed him. His father was bigger, but he was working with the sluggish reflexes of a drunk. He had raised the bottle to take a swing at him, but he was too slow. Silence was on him. He hit him with a solid right that knocked his head up against the wall, staggering him. He rained down blows on him with such ferocity that a bullet to the temple may have been less painful.

Catching himself, before he turned the beating into murder, he stopped and looked down at the battered man he resembled so much. He was beaten, literally, yet he still had the strength to breathe out curses. Silence just shook his head in disgust.

Becoming aware of other's presence, he looked at the entrance to the kitchen where his little brother and their mother were just standing there, shocked. Walking towards them, he looked into her eyes expecting to see something, but there was nothing there for him. "Come on," he said, putting his arm around Jerome's shoulder.

As he was reaching down to pick up Jerome's bag from the front door, he spotted his father charging him with a knife. Turning around just in time, he caught his arm in mid-air. Struggling over the knife, they fell to the floor. Finally wrestling the knife away, Silence pinned him down and planted the knife in his chest.

Climbing off the dying body, he calmly went outside and sat on the front porch as he had as a child when he listened to his father beat his mother. Not willing to look at the terrified look on his little brother's tear-streaked face, he stared off into the sunset. This time he was listening to the sirens drawing near.

CHAPTER 3

2015

"Rodger's Auto Parts. How may I help you?"

"Detrick?" inquired the caller, somewhat suspiciously.

"Wh-what?" Detrick stammered, looking around to make sure his father wasn't lurking. "Who is this?"

"It's Scam, fool! I need my money! TODAY!"

"Man, what are you doing calling me at work, dude? You tripping," he whispered.

"I ain't gotta call at all, homie. I could come down there in person and trip, feel me?" he threatened.

"Alright, man. Chill out. But for real, I told you I won't have it until Friday."

"You don't seem to get it, homie. Two weeks ago, you told me Friday. When Friday came around, you told next Friday. Now you're telling me this Friday. You sound like an Ice Cube sequel, man. I'm done with that. You gon have my money tonight, or I'll be there bright and early in the morning to discuss this business with your pops. You feeling me?"

"Yeah, I got you," he muttered, slamming the phone down.

"Boy, what's wrong with you? This is a place of business, and broken phones come out of paychecks," his dad said as he walked in.

"My bad, Pops. Female problems."

He watched his father turn around and walk off with a disgusted look on his face. It was a look he had often received, but it still hurt. Detrick admired his father more than he would probably ever know, and his approval was something he desperately desired. But for some reason, he could never do enough or seem to get anything right. And now this.

How it had gotten that far, he didn't know. But a one night "experiment" with cocaine at a party, chasing after a woman, had blossomed into a $3,600 debt. One he couldn't afford. Although his father owned a business, and he was sure his family would pay off the debt to keep him from being harmed, he felt he would never be able to face his father as a man after that.

As he made his way through a busy workday, he tried to keep his mind off Scam's threat. But how could he? And how could he have been stupid enough to get himself caught up with someone who was nicknamed "Scam"? If he didn't have the money by tonight, dude definitely would approach his father with it in the morning. He thought about killing him, but he didn't even have the heart to fight him, much less take his life. He had even considered going to his sister for help, but she had been sheltered. She didn't understand the criminal elements. She'd probably want to call the police. So, whatever he chose to do, he was on his own.

Sometime around one in the afternoon he decided to take his lunch break. He wished he had opened that bank account his sister had suggested, but he probably would have overdrawn it by now anyway. He had called a couple of his so-called partners to see if he could borrow the money from them, but all he had gotten was the promise of $100 from one of them who seemed to have forgotten that he already owed Detrick $200 from six months ago.

As he sat down to eat at one of his favorite soul food restaurants, an article in a newspaper left at the table caught his attention. And as he kept reading, an idea of a way out began to take shape. It was risky… even foolish. It guaranteed to cause his family some grief, but it would also spare him the shame of what he had gotten himself entangled in. After all, the night was gradually approaching, and he was running out of options.

At six that evening, he and his father closed the shop, going their separate ways. Detrick went home, changed clothes, and downed a couple shots of vodka. He called a lady friend he had been fooling with who lived down the street, and asked if he could use her car for a few hours to run some errands.

"Run some errands!? What's wrong with your car?" she asked, with a little attitude.

"On my way home from work the brakes started acting up," he lied.

"Boy, you work in an auto parts store. How your brakes gon be acting up?"

"I can't get em fixed until the morning," he responded, agitated that he was having to deal with her right now. "Look, I'm tired, and I've had a long day. Either you are or you ain't?"

"Boy, no you didn't run that lame game on me. I haven't heard from you in two weeks and when I do, it's only to use my car. Stop it!"

"So?"

"Yeaaah, I guess so. But you better fill my tank back up, and I bet not hear about you having any of your lil freaks in my car!"

"Come on. You know better than that."

"Yeah, whatever."

After walking down the street to get the car, Detrick pulled up to the back of Rodger's Auto Parts. Nervously, he pulled out a small bag of cocaine and took a few hits. With new-found courage, he got out of the car, checked the scene, and opened the back door with his key.

Hurriedly, he made his way to the safe in the office. He had memorized the combination from watching his father over the years. *Why had I done that?* he wondered.

Looking into the safe, he blasphemously thanked God they had been so busy at work over the past week that his father hadn't been able to leave and make a deposit in the bank. So, there was more than enough money there to take care of the debt. He stuffed it into his coat pocket and started to close the door of the safe when something caught his eye. It was the deed to the store. And right under his father's name was his own.

In that moment, he almost did the right thing because that piece of paper was proof that his father loved him and believed in him. That love could get them through this. He could always earn his father's trust and respect back. *We could get through this,* he thought. But he was not in his right mind. Fear, shame, and cocaine were controlling him. So, he threw the deed on the floor, poured the rest of the contents of the safe out, and went on to the next part of his plan.

Going into the storage room, he came out carrying two jugs of gasoline. He really hadn't wanted to burn the store down, but he had to cover up the crime. Besides, his father had insurance on the place. He would build a bigger store! He sat one of the jugs on the floor, unscrewed the cap, and knocked it over, spilling the flammable liquid all over the floor. With the other jug he made a trail to the back door and pulled a book of matches out of his pants pocket. He considered doing the right thing once more, but instead, he lit a match, and he ran towards the car as fast as he could.

Unfortunately for him, he ran right into the hands of the police, who had been running the tags on the car. In his haste, and drug-induced state of mind, he had forgotten to punch in the code on the security system his father had recently installed, which triggered a silent alarm.

Sitting in the back of the police car in handcuffs, watching the fire he had set destroy a part of his family's dream, he wondered, *what would Pops think of me now?* And all he could feel was an overwhelming sense of the very shame he had been trying to avoid.

CHAPTER 4

2017

"Thank you, baby," JG said, stuffing the money into his pocket and flashing a smile full of gold teeth. He was a pretty boy from head to toe. Slim, athletic build, light-skinned, with a head full of waves. Fresh dressed, with J's on his feet to match.

"It's cool, baby. You know I got you," said the short, country-thick female he had met in the club a few months ago. "Are you coming back through later on?" she asked.

"I'ma try. I got a lot of business to take care of," he smoothly stated. "But if I don't make it, you know I love you, right?"

"I know, baby. I love you, too," she responded, leaning back on the front door, blocking his exit. "But I *really* want to see you tonight," she emphasized with a sultry look in her eyes.

"I know, and if I can, I will. But if you hold me hostage now, I won't have time to do everything I need to so I can make it back."

"Okay," she reluctantly relented, opening the door.

JG gave her a kiss on the lips, a slap on her luscious backside, and strolled through the apartment complex to where his truck was parked. There was a pretty, tall, chocolate Amazon of a woman parked next to him getting into her car. Not willing to miss out on an opportunity to add to his "stable" he turned on the charm and got her number. He pulled off in his money green SUV, thinking to himself, *Now, that's pimping!* Well, not exactly pimping, because his women weren't selling anything! He bet not even hear about them talking too long to another dude. In his own way, he loved em. All of em! But they did "break him off," so he was no less than a playa.

As he was riding, trying to figure out what to do with the rest of the day, he got a call from his cousin, Tina. "Hello?"

"What's up, trick!" she said, jokingly. "What you got going on?"

"Please! You better recognize a playa," he shot back.

"Boy, please. Anyways, what you bout to do?"

"I was just trying to figure that out."

"Well, come and take me to work so I can pick up my check."

"Man, that don't go straight into your account?"

"Not where I work."

"You need to tell them folks it's time to upgrade. They living in the stone age."

"I don't care what they do as long as I get mine. You coming, ain't you?"

"Yeah. I was wondering who was gon fill the tank up for me today. I'll be there in bout ten minutes," he said, hanging up the phone.

Hopping onto the freeway, he thought about Tina and her mother, Trish. Other than his son, two-year old J Jr., and his child's mother, Jessica, they were the only other people in the world who he knew truly loved him. His father was in the feds now. He used to be heavy in the dope game, and his idea of love was buying you something he wanted you to have. Not spending time with you or anything meaningful. So, JG grew up learning how to be a man from his father's "friends," who were playas, pimps, and hustlers.

Now, his mother was something altogether different. She was an ex-junkie/ prostitute, and those lifestyles had drained all the love out of her. She was a beautiful woman, and after she had gotten off the dope, it was hard for any man to resist her allure. To this day, his father swore that the only reason she had gotten pregnant was to trap him up.

Because the only true love she had was money, which his father could provide!

As he pulled into his aunt's driveway, Tina was already on her way out of the door. She was tall, athletic, and pretty. When they were young, they had a "kissing cousins" relationship until Trish caught them and whooped it out of them. After that, they became the best of friends.

"Man, I hope you spending some of that paycheck at the beauty shop!" JG said, smiling.

"Shut up, boy!" she exclaimed, pulling her baseball cap down on her head. "We had a meet yesterday, punk," she said, punching him in the arm. She ran the 200m hurdles for the University track team.

JG backed out of the driveway and hit the road.

"Why you didn't call me and let me know? You know I would've been there to support you."

"Support me? Yeah, right! You would've been posted up at the finish line trying to run your lame game on every girl who was too tired to diss you."

"You tripping. I always let em catch their breath before I put the mack down. I ain't trying to kill nobody."

"Boy, you stupid!" she said, laughing. "Anyway, you need to stop worrying about all them skanks and spend some time with the mother of your child. She's the one who's going to be there no matter what."

Tina and Jessica were good friends. She had introduced the two of them, hoping a good girl like Jessica would slow him down. But instead of slowing down, all he had done was gotten her pregnant and become more of a slut.

"Jessica's my girl. I care about her. You know that. But she thought she was getting a husband or something. I'm not on that. I'm a playa. Period!"

"Man, whatever. You're full of it, that's what you are."

This was the one thing that caused friction in their relationship. It wasn't just the fact that she felt responsible for introducing them, but they also had a son, and his whorish ways created problems with Jessica that kept him away from his child. They were both to blame. Jessica was grown, but he had led her to believe it was something that it wasn't.

After that exchange they made the rest of the short drive with very little communication, listening to music. When they were almost there, he asked how his Aunt Trish was doing.

"She's good. They've been working her like a dog at the hospital. She's hardly been home all week, but she called and said she would be in later. I'll tell her you asked about her."

"I might stop by for a little while. I ain't seen her in a couple of weeks."

"Do that," she said, conspiringly adding, "and I'll see if Jessica and J Jr. can make it over too."

He shook his head, laughing. "You messed up in the head, cousin."

"I guess it runs in the family."

"Right," he agreed. "Anyway, where is your car?"

"My husband wrecked his, so he's using mine to get back and forth to work."

"Oh, it's your husband now!"

"You heard what I said!"

"Well, you need to tell your husband he owes me Uber fare."

"I know you weren't serious about needing some gas money."

Pulling into the driveway he put the car in the park. "Come on, girl. You know my women take care of they business."

Unable to conceal her smile, she screamed, "Boy, I can't stand you!" and got out of the car.

"I love you, too!" he screamed, backing out of the driveway, smiling.

JG was determined to make it out there to see Aunt Trish later that night. But after napping for a few hours and taking a shower, he decided to go to Bruiser's first and see if he could "get some get back" at the dice game. A few nights ago, they had hit him for almost three racks, and he wasn't about to take that lying down. So, he figured he would take $1,500 with him and see how it went.

He arrived at around 7:30 pm. Now, as business-like as "Bruiser's" may sound, it was actually a two-story, four-bedroom house down the street from the projects where illegal gambling and back door weed sales took place. Dice, cards, numbers, etc., every room was occupied, and "security" made sure things didn't get out of hand… and, to keep the robbers at bay, of course.

JG was a regular, so as he walked through the house everybody spoke. Many of the old-head hustlers called him "Lil Money D," after his father. By the time he made it to the dice game, it was already jumping. There was a pool table in the middle of the room with about twelve dudes gathered around. There were a few heavy hitters in the room, so there were large amounts of money being bet around the table. JG found himself getting excited. He loved to gamble.

He had planned on leaving around ten o'clock. However, three and a half hours after he got there, he was up $4,500. He knew he should stop while he was ahead because he couldn't keep passing, but the problem with that line of reasoning was that he did: tens and fours, fives and nines, sixes and eights, sevens and elevens out the door. Tonight, he couldn't miss. If he had just had one small stretch where things weren't going his way, he'd be gone by now. But until then, he was going to ride this thing out.

Fortunately, or unfortunately, depending on your perspective, a half hour later he had such a stretch. He missed on a five, an eight, and a four. The next time his shot came around, he bet over $1,100 that he would hit before he ever saw the point. He rolled another eight, bet $500 more and crapped out the next roll. He took that as a sign and gracefully bowed out, up about $5,700. Saying his "I'll holler at ya's" and giving dap, he made his way to the front door. When he was just about to walk out, he was stopped by a slightly older cat he had been gambling with.

"Hey, J-Gizzle!"

"What's good?" he asked, alertly. This dude ran with a click who was always on shyst.

"Check this out, homie. Ya'll did me bad back there, and I was hoping I could hold like a G to try to get back. I'll get it back to you when I can."

"Yeah, I ain't got it like that. But I can hit you with a couple hundred on the strength." JG had caught the threat in his words and his eyes, but he was far from a coward.

"For real, homie! I told you I'll get it back to you...." He let out a sardonic chuckle and smiled. "Alright, man. That's cool. I guess I'll have to work with that."

Their brief exchange had drawn the attention of one the "security personnel" who came over to investigate.

"Everything straight?"

"Yeah, bruh," the shysty dude cunningly announced, "I'm always straight."

"What about you, Lil Money D, you straight?" he asked with concern.

"I'm good," JG said, good-naturedly. "I'ma make a quick phone call and get out of here."

Reaching into his left pocket he came out with a small roll of bills. Peeling off two Ben Franklins, he handed them to the shysty dude.

"Yeah, I 'preciate that, *homie*" he said, not trying to disguise the sarcasm.

JG chose to ignore it. He called Tina to see if they were awake.

"What's up trick!" she answered.

"Your 'husband' the trick," he shot back.

"Whatever. Anyway, I thought you were coming over?"

"That's why I'm calling, to see if y'all still up."

"Mama and your son sleep, but me and your future wife up." He could tell that she was smiling on the other end of the phone. "Are you coming?"

"Yeah, I'm on my way. Yall still got something to eat?"

"Of course! You got something to smoke?"

"Of course! I'll be there in bout twenty minutes."

"Alright. We love you, don't we Jessica?" He hung up.

As was his habit, he parked his truck down the street in front of a female friend's house. The hood was dark and walking around with chunks in your pocket was like an invitation. Once he made it to his truck, he thought he was safe. But just as he was opening the door he saw the reflection of a dark figure with a gun in his hand coming from behind him. Reaching under the driver's seat, he grabbed his strap and turned around firing. There were no warning shots in the streets.

Seeing his would-be jacker fall to the ground clutching his stomach, JG jumped into his ride and smashed off. Unable to calm his nerves, he ran into a blue Mustang at a stop sign on the corner, but he kept going. He had one destination in mind, and he wasn't stopping until he got there.

Pulling into his Aunt Trish's driveway, he turned off the car and just sat there for a moment. *DAMN!* Everything was going good. Why did dude try me like that? I wonder if he's dead? All of this was going through his mind as Tina came out on the front porch, waving for him to come in. He could see Jessica standing in the doorway. He finally composed himself enough to get out of the truck and go into the house, to spend some quality time with his family, hoping it wasn't the last time he'd be doing so for a long time. Now he wished he had come sooner, before his son went to sleep.

CHAPTER 5

2020- Present Day

"Marcus Jones; thirty-one cell; visit!" screams the c/o working the unit.

For Marcus, it was difficult to understand how he had ended up here. Just a year ago his future had been promising. He was a bright high-school graduate on his way to the University of Tennessee, and happily in love with a young woman he *thought* loved him just as much. But in one night, due to one tragically bad decision, the promise was lost. Now he lived in a nightmare.

As he made his way to the visitation gallery, he again examined the compound that would be his home for the next five years. It was a series of dull, gray buildings. There was a chow hall that was too small for the number of people fed there, and unsanitary in ways he tried not to think about. A gym that hosted more gang meetings than athletic events and was undoubtedly the epicenter of fights in the prison. A school building with a less than twenty percent graduation rate, a chapel that was either overlooked or undervalued, and sadly, a law library that, more often than not, was only occupied by two or three prisoners who actually utilized it for the purpose intended. And this was despite the fact that every unit housed numerous inmates who were serving sentences in excess of twenty-five years. Some were serving sentences in the hundreds. Shaking his head, Marcus walked into the v.g.

After a routine pat-down search by the visitation officer, he surveyed the room and spotted his family. As expected, everyone had made the trip. That is, everyone who hadn't already jumped ship. Everyone who mattered. It was his third month in prison after spending the previous eight trying to mentally and emotionally prepare himself for what he thought prison life meant. This was his first visit with the whole family. His father had already come a few times by himself, but his mother and sister had just built up the strength to face him under these circumstances.

Looking into his little sister's eyes, he could see that she was doing her best to hold in a fountain of tears as she nervously looked around, so he quickly wrapped his arms around her to assure her that everything was going to be okay. Though he was not quite so sure that it would be himself. After comforting his sister, he turned to look at his mother. She had been affected more than anyone by this ordeal. It appeared to him that she had aged dramatically since he last saw her. Her eyes weren't as lively, and her face wasn't as joyful. She was visibly hurting on the inside.

Embracing his mother, Marcus wanted to cry himself. How had this happened to such a lovely family? He had tried so hard to do things the right way, still he had hurt them so deeply. Stepping away from his mother, he looked at his father; strong and confident, a man of faith and integrity, the soul of the family, his best friend. Hugging his dad always made him feel better, as it did now.

Sitting down, the family did their best to enjoy the visit. It was Marcus' birthday. Conversation was strained, but they made it through nearly three hours before parting ways again. After the visit, Marcus went straight to his cell. Instead of feeling better, he felt worse. A few minutes later Silence walked in.

"What's good, celly-cell?" he asked, genuinely concerned. "I thought you went to visit to see your family? You look like you've been to a funeral. What's up, man? You good?"

"It was a funeral," Marcus said, somberly, rolling over to face the wall.

Silence was never one to push someone into a conservation they didn't want to have, so he left it at that. However, about an hour later, as Silence was studying his business course, Marcus was ready to talk.

"Hey Silence, you busy?"

"Not too busy. What's up?"

"Man, we've been in the cell together for almost three months now. Why haven't you ever asked me about my charge?"

Silence put down his pencil, closed the book, stood up, and looked into Marcus' eyes as he sat on the top bunk.

"I haven't asked for the same reasons you haven't asked about mine," he said. "It's none of my business. Plus, I got my own demons to deal with."

"So, what? You don't wanna hear about it?" Marcus asked, desperately wanting to share it.

"I didn't say that lil bruh. I said it wasn't necessary for me to know. But if you need to get it off your chest, get it off."

"Alright," he said, exhaling. "Well, I already told you I was on my way to UT before I caught this charge. My identical twin brother was going too. On the night of our high school graduation, we were out riding." He choked up a little. It was painful just thinking about it. Talking about it felt like torture, but he had to let it out.

"We had never really messed with drugs. We had smoked weed one time and got so high we were scared to go home so we tried to 'hide' from our parents over our auntie's house. When we passed out, she called them, and... well," he paused and smiled, enjoying the memory.

"But for some stupid reason," he continued, "we wanted to 'turn up' for graduation.

So, we bought a couple of pills, a few blunts, and some Hen. We were gon take our girls to the room, pop the pills and ... you know. Celebrate." Now his eyes were watery, He couldn't help it. It hurt.

"But on the way to the room... I don't know what happened... I had hit a blunt and drank a little... but not enough to... Anyway, I got dizzy and ran through a red light..." The tears were pouring out now, but he went on.

"A truck smashed right into the passenger side, killing my dude, instantly. Snapped his neck." He lay back on the bed, sobbing bitterly. Silence turned away from him and walked to the door. He felt like an intruder.

About thirty seconds later Marcus sat back up, face streaked with tears. And then he said, as if to himself, "And all I walked away with was a few scrapes and bruises."

Silence stood there for a while, looking out of the door window. He understood. He'd been there himself. He'd felt the regret and guilt of the decisions he had made in life.

"Look, man. I know it's easier said than done, but you can't beat yourself up. You didn't try to do it. It was an accident," he concluded, trying to comfort Marcus.

"Yeah, I know. But you don't understand. It was my twin brother," Marcus said, sadly. "And every time I look in the mirror, I see his face. Every time my family looks at me, they see his face. I'm a constant reminder of what we've lost. And it's killing us. My mama could hardly look at me. She's not getting much sleep. My little sister couldn't *stop* looking at me, but she wasn't seeing me, she was seeing, Malcom, my twin. And my dad is trying to be strong for all of us, but I can tell it's wearing him down. Man! I just don't know what to do!" He finished, defeated.

After a minute or so without a word, Silence made a final effort to help.

"Lil bruh, I'm the wrong one to be giving you advice about family matters. I gave up on that a long time ago. But I will tell you that, as much as I understand, I believe you're being too hard on yourself. You were just a kid. And it was an accident caused by a decision made by the both of you."

"Yeah, but accidents still have consequences."

"Sure, they do. Sometimes extreme. But a life full of guilt doesn't have to be one of them. It takes another bad decision for that to happen."

CHAPTER 6

Boss was sitting on a milk crate cushioned with blankets in front of his cell door reading the newspaper when JG walked up.

"What's good, Bossman?" JG said, giving him some dap.

"Just taking in my daily dose of the world. What's happening, J?"

"Man, you know me. Trying to get it."

Boss folded his newspaper and sat it on the floor.

"Yeah, I hear you, 'trying to get it.' You better reconsider, lil bruh. You gon end up losing more than you gain." He didn't play around when it came to shining light on the true nature of the game. "Anyway, what's up? You don't holler at me unless you need something."

For some reason he couldn't explain, Boss had taken an instant liking to JG. He was sure that if he didn't slow down, he would soon crash out. But he had an energy about him that made him easy to like.

"Ah man, don't be like that, Boss. You know I'm constantly trying to soak up some of that wisdom you got," he said, smiling.

"Man, cut it out! You don't want wisdom. You want that nonsense we call the game. I almost gotta force feed you wisdom. So, what do you want this time?"

"Man, you cold," he said, feigning hurt. "But I do need some sandwich bags, big bruh," he continued, grinning.

Boss just shook his head. What could he do? If he said no, he'd just get them elsewhere. And at least it gave him a chance to hit him with the truth. "Yeah, man. Come on in."

Now, the majority of prison cells you go into resemble a bathroom equipped with shelves for clothing, food, and entertainment, as well as twin bunk beds. But Boss' cell had a completely different look and feel to it. It was more like a library. Every inch of shelf space that didn't have clothes on it was occupied by either a book or some other form of literature, Bibles and law books, mostly. But his interests went much deeper. He was the best example of a Christian that JG has ever known, in or out of prison. Yet he had taken the time to study everything from Islam to Scientology. He has an associate's degree in business management and was in the process of acquiring a degree in psychology. He also had two unfinished novels he was writing. All of this, tucked into a two-man bathroom.

As is always the case, JG was amazed that one person could read so much. "For real, Boss," he said with amusement, "if you keep this up, you gon be sleeping on books."

"Yeah, I know. But it'll probably be more comfortable than these old mats we got."

"Man, what you said!" Boss had always encouraged him to read more, so he grabbed Dennis Kimbro's *Think and Grow Rich: A Black Choice* off the shelf. "What is this one about, Boss?" he asked, flipping through the pages.

Glancing over, Boss nodded his head in approval. "Yeah, you'll like that one. I got turned on to that years ago. Basically, it's a call to reach your fullest potential by changing your view of yourself. Black people, especially black men, have been trained, even indoctrinated, to see ourselves from an inferior perspective, especially intellectually. So, we limit ourselves to rapping, playing sports, and 'trappin' as you call it. But if we learn to see ourselves as business owners, politicians, judges, lawyers, authors, whatever, it'll change our ambitions and transform our culture. It all starts in there," Boss emphasized, pointing at his temple.

"That's deep," JG pondered.

"It is. Consider this: What is the greatest thing you ever achieved?"

"My son," he said proudly.

"True that. But as a man we have this drive in us to achieve and conquer the world. Have you ever personally accomplished anything that gave you that type of fulfillment?"

"I broke up a few big dice games. And I slept with some of the baddest females in my city."

"That's exactly what I'm talking about, lil bruh! That might mean something to a lot of people. It obviously means something to you. But when you sincerely and honestly think about it, how poorly motivated and how low must a man's expectations in life be, when breaking up thousand-dollar crap games and sleeping with hundred-dollar women, who also have low expectations, is something worthy of being labeled an accomplishment?"

"So, you're saying I have low expectations?"

"No, you're saying it!"

"How so?"

Boss thought for a second. "Ok. I believe I saw you with an *Entrepreneur* magazine earlier this week, right?"

"Yeah."

"Do you actually read em?"

"Some of it. My auntie Trish got me a subscription to it," he replied nonchalantly.

"You should thank her and show your appreciation by reading it. All of it."

"Yeah, I know."

"Anyway, what kind of stuff were they talking about?"

"Business. A lot of tech stuff. New apps, things like that."

"No dice games. No 'bad' women?"

"Alright," JG said, chuckling. "I feel you."

"I hope so, little bruh. Your auntie sent you that magazine because she loves you and sees something in you... who you could be if you started looking at yourself from the right perspective. God's perspective."

"Come on, Bossman. What's God got to do with owning a business?"

"Everything! Whether people acknowledge it or not, without God there is no Microsoft, Apple, Google, Facebook, or anything else."

"How so?" JG inquired.

"Because ain't no intelligence apart from God. And without that God-given intelligence, which had to be nurtured and honored, of course, there is no business. Deuteronomy 8:18 says, but you shall remember the LORD your God, for it is He who is giving you the power or wisdom, knowledge, ability to obtain wealth..."

"Alright, Bossman! That's all the preaching I can handle in one session. Stand down!" he said. He slick enjoyed these conversations in doses.

"Man, you a radical Christian! Whenever God do let you up out of here, the devil got problems. You gon be out there on the block preaching business ethics from the Bible while everybody else out there trappin." They both smiled at that. "And look, let me get one of those cheeseburgers you got in the cooler before I roll. I can't be reading nothing this heavy on an empty stomach."

At that, Boss couldn't help but laugh. He reached inside the cooler and grabbed one of the sandwiches he had wrapped in a zip lock.

"Here, man. Get out of my cell before you take me for everything I got."

"Appreciate you, big homie."

"Alright, J. Enjoy the book."

"Alright, Bossman."

✝

Later that day JG was sitting on the bunk in his cell reading when someone knocked on the door. Looking up, he waved him in.

"What's good, J?"

"What's up, Lil D? I got some killa, fool!"

"Yeah, I heard. And you already know I need a bag." He spotted the book lying on the bed next to him. "I see you been over there hollering at Boss."

JG picked the book up. "Yeah. You know what, homie? I had never in my life read a book until I met Boss. When I get up with him, dude so deep with it, he make you wanna know more. Plus, I know he got my best interest at heart. He genuinely cares, man. I can tell."

At that, an awkward silence ensued. Each man was in his own thoughts. Thinking about their fathers. For JG, thinking about his dad didn't hurt until he thought about his own son. And then he was keenly aware of the way he'd felt as a child, not having his pops around. Now he was taking his son through the same thing. Lil D, on the other hand, had never questioned his father's love. He just found it difficult to understand the conditions of it. They were two different people, so how in the world had his father expected him to live up to his image. He just didn't get it. And it cut too deep trying.

"Check this out, J," he said, relieving them both of their reveries. "Let me get one now, and I'll get the rest when I bring you the numbers." He needed something to take his thoughts elsewhere.

Reaching into his pocket, JG pulled out a bag of weed about the size of a ping-pong ball and handed it to Lil D. "Here. I know you good for it, homie."

"That's what's up, J. I'll get at you after my sister gets off work."

"Bet," he said, still thinking about his son.

That night, after a serious smoke session, Lil D's thoughts were still centered around his father. He hadn't seen him or spoken to him since the day of his sentencing hearing. He had wanted to apologize, but he had done that so many times over the years, only to make the same mistakes again, or worse, that the words just wouldn't come out. How could he say, "Hey Pops, my bad for robbing you and burning down the business you labored for decades to build to support my drug habit?" How could his father forgive that? So, for five years now, not a word was spoken between them.

Leaving the solitude of his cell, and his thoughts, he stepped out onto the top walk and looked around. Controlled chaos at its best... or worst. *I guess it depended on who you asked.* At this time of day nearly everyone was back from work and school, so the pod was buzzing. Sixty-four cells, one hundred and twenty-eight prisoners. There was movement everywhere. It almost seemed as if the spade table was having a shouting match with the domino table. And they were all shouting over the new Yo Gotti beating out of one of one of the hustler's cell. Chaos!

Walking down the stairs to the phone module located in the middle of the pod, Lil D dialed his sister's number. *If it wasn't for big sis,* he pondered, *I don't know how I would make it in here.* She had been deeply saddened and hurt by what had happened. But her pain didn't just come from what he had done. It also came from the fact that he hadn't felt like he could come to her for help in his time of need. Not to mention that all of this had practically torn the family apart.

After accepting the collect call, she excitedly screamed into the phone, "Happy Birthday, lil bruh!" She always knew how to make him feel better.

"Appreciate it, sis. What's going on?"

"Nothing. Just got in from work. Getting ready to cook a lil something for dinner."

"What you cooking?" he inquired. He always wanted to know, and she always looked forward to telling him. It was one of their things.

"I'ma keep it simple tonight. Turkey cheeseburgers and potato wedges. I gotta work on these designs, so I don't have time to cut up like I normally do."

"What you working on now?"

"A device that automatically puts out engine fires."

"Oh yeah?"

"Yeah. It's still in the early stages. But it's needed. And when I put it together, bank!"

"I hear you, sis. That's what's up!"

"Thank you. Anyway, do you still need me to do that?"

"Yeah. I appreciate it, sis."

"Man, I know! And I told you, you ain't gotta keep telling me that." For some reason, it annoyed her. "Anyway, how has your day been? How does it feel to be thirty?"

"Not too much different than the last few. Looking forward to celebrating one with y'all in the future."

"You'll be here soon," she said, encouraging him.

"So how is Mama doing?"

"She's good. I gave her the letter and card you sent. She said she sent you some money and stamps."

"Yeah, I got it," he said, in a reflective tone.

"Why don't you call her, bruh?"

"I'd love to, sis. But it caused a big argument between her and Daddy last time, and I don't wanna take her through that again."

"Bruh, Daddy is not tripping about you calling. He's tripping on the fact that you still haven't apologized for what you did. To tell you the truth, I'm tripping on that."

"Come on, sis. You know I'm sorry for what I did."

"Yeah, I do. Mama knows and Daddy knows too. But bruh, you eventually gotta grow up, and face him man to man."

"I know, sis," he said with great conviction, "but how? I been messing up my whole life. And I just don't see how he can forgive me for what I did." He sounded defeated.

"Detrick, I love you. We all love you. And no matter how bad it gets at times, we were raised in a household that believes that love covers a multitude of sins. So, the problem is not that Daddy hasn't forgiven you. The problem is that you won't forgive yourself."

CHAPTER 7

Prison is a lot like the free world, after a curfew has been declared. During the day, you worked and went to school and enjoyed recreation or leisure time as you desired. Or, like millions of people on the outside, you simply did nothing but exist. But at 9:00 pm, all movement ceased. So, the thing to do was find a routine that would get you through the day.

Silence had a routine that has worked for years now. He got up at five in the morning, and from 5:30am to 7:00am he spent time on academic pursuits. He was presently working on a Business Management Correspondence course. He chose this time because nearly everyone in the pod is sleeping or just waking up, so it was about as quiet as it gets in prison. From 8:00am to 12:00 noon he worked as a writer for the prison newsletter that he jokingly referred to as *Nothing but Times*. He usually worked out sometime in the afternoon, and then he was free to do whatever he chose.

As usual, that afternoon he was working out with Boss under the weight shack. Even at fifty years old Boss was a beast. That's why Silence chose to work out with him. He never had to worry about not being pushed.

"Come on, man! Get that off your chest! Up! Up! I see you! Push!" Boss screamed, as the three hundred- and fifteen-pounds Silence was bench pressing inched its way up.

"Ahhh!" he roared, with veins bulging out of his sweat-drenched face as he got closer to locking his arms out.

"You got it, E! That's all you! Come on, man!"

Silence finally locked his arms out and Boss helped him rack it.

"That's what I'm talking about, man! That's how you finish a workout!" Boss exclaimed as they stripped the weight from the bar and got ready to walk some laps around the yard.

"Boss, you missed your calling, man. You should've been a drill sergeant. Or a torturer." He wiped the sweat from his face with a towel and took a sip from his water bottle. "I wouldn't have even tried three fifteen after that chest routine we just did if you hadn't been barking at me."

"Yeah, well it's obvious I chose the wrong line of work," Boss responded with a smile. "But you could've got that three weeks ago. You been beasting. You just cheat yourself sometimes," he said grinning.

"Yeah, right!" Silence replied with a similar grin.

Walking around the yard was a daily liberty they both enjoyed. They always allowed themselves a few minutes to clear their minds before speaking. Boss had always considered the big yard to be somewhat of a sanctuary. It was the biggest open space in prison, so it afforded you the privilege of getting off to yourself without intrusion. For a couple of hours, at least.

Rounding the bend by the softball field, the tranquility was broken by Silence. "My lil brother wrote me again," he said nonchalantly.

"Yeah?"

"Yeah. He sent me some bread, even though I keep sending it back."

"Send it to me," Boss said, playfully.

Silence gave him a look that said, "For real, man?"

"What? Don't look at me like that, E. I ain't beefing with him."

"Come on, man. Don't do that. You know how I am about this," Silence said, trying to look as serious as he sounded. But for some reason, it never worked on Boss.

"Alright, man. Don't turn green on me. You know I'd never disrespect you, lil bruh. But E, how long are you going to hold on to this? You treating it like those were normal circumstances or something. He was twelve years old. He messed up. And he has apologized a thousand times. But you won't forgive him. You act like he was some street dude. Come on, bruh."

"Yeah, but he still should've known better."

"How, E? He saw his father get butchered."

"Man, that dude wasn't no father!" Silence said, vehemently.

Boss let him cool down a little before going on. Family was a touchy subject. Even when someone let you into that area of their life, there were still boundaries.

"Maybe not, lil bruh. From what you've told me he was a drunk, verbally and physically abusive, and unaffectionate, even toward family."

"Like I said, man, that dude was not a father."

"Well, to you he wasn't. You were old enough to comprehend just how much he fell short of the values and responsibilities a father is supposed to embody. But not Jerome, all he knew was that his father was a drunk, abusive, and unaffectionate. To him, he was a bad father, but still his father. And due to some unfortunate circumstances, you killed him. Right or wrong, from your brother's point of view he didn't deserve to die that day. So just let it go and move on."

"It's not that easy, Boss. I killed for him, and he turned his back on me."

"Did you? And is that really what he did?"

"Yeah, and that's exactly what he did!"

"Well, I can't make you see it how I see it. But you're one of the few people I've spoken to about my family. And believe me, there's not a day that goes by that I don't miss them. But there is nothing I can do about it." Boss paused and looked off into the distance.

"But if I could, nothing... not who is at fault or anything petty like that, would keep me from them. Nothing!"

They had stopped walking, and now both men were standing there gazing through the fence. And based on the look in their eyes, they were hundreds, perhaps thousands of miles away and many years in the past, in their minds.

Placing his hand on the younger man's shoulder, Boss turned to Silence with tears welling up in his eyes and said, "Fix it, lil bruh. Because if you don't, you'll end up regretting it for the rest of your life."

✝

Jerome had just secured his son in the car seat when he felt the barrel of a gun shoved into the back of his head. "Don't play, homie!" screamed an irate teenager with braids.

"Please! You can have the car, my wallet, everything. Just let me and my son go."

"Shut up, busta!" yelled another dread-locked youth, hitting Jerome in the head with a gun nearly half as big as he was. "I'ma ask you one time and one time only: where the money and dope at?"

"Where the what at? Look, you got the wrong man. I don't know anything about no dope or drug money or any of that. I'm a school teacher." Jerome was in a panic. He could see his son in the car seat crying, wondering what was going on. Dreadlocks hit him again, knocking him to the ground.

"Ain't you that nigga Silence's brother?"

"What? Look, you got it all wrong."

"And you don't know nothing?" he asked, sarcastically.

"Listen," Jerome cried, "you don't understand. I'm not in that life. I don't know anything. Please, man, just let me and my son go," he pleaded.

Dreadlocks looked at his partner in crime. "You know what, dawg? I believe this fool."

"So, what we gon do?"

Dreadlocks looked back to Jerome. "I believe you, homie I do." Jerome felt a moment of relief. "But my big brother didn't get a chance to beg for his life and neither do you." So, he mechanically pulled the trigger and shot Jerome in the face.

"No!" Silence screamed, jerking out of his sleep, tears and sweat streaming down his face.

"You alright, bruh?" asked Marcus, who had been awakened by the scream.

"Yeah, I'm good, homie."

"Alright, man," and he was right back out.

But Silence knew he wouldn't sleep for the rest of the night. Boss' words from last week were echoing in his head, "Fix it, lil bruh. Or you'll end up regretting it for the rest of your life."

Turning on the lamp next to the desk, he got up and put enough water in the hot pot for a cup of coffee. Since he couldn't sleep, he figured he may as well get some work done. He intended to do his schoolwork, but he couldn't concentrate. The dream was too vivid, too real. Almost surreal.

Feeling uneasy about the situation, he decided to do something he hadn't done in a while; read the Bible. He still hadn't determined if he actually believed everything it said. But he did believe it presented some truths worth practicing. Opening "The Good Book," he turned to Matthew 6 and read the Lord's Prayer. Reading on, however, he saw something he couldn't overlook. Matthew 6:14-15,

"14) For if you forgive men their trespasses, your heavenly father will also forgive you:

15) But if you do not forgive others their trespasses, neither will your father forgive your trespasses."

Man! God sure knows how to get your attention. *If anybody needs to be forgiven, it's me,* he thought. He had done things in his life that he himself considered to be unforgivable. So, with those scriptures, and Boss' words in mind, he sat down at the desk at three o'clock in the morning and wrote a letter.

Jerome,

Man! I really don't know where to start. I never thought I'd be writing this letter or having this conversation. Period! I loved you, bruh! I loved you so much that I would've done anything for you. I did!

But you repaid me with what I consider the ultimate betrayal. You got on the stand and told them folks I didn't have to kill him. That I chose to! Man, the only choice I made in that moment was to protect my lil brother from a drunk who was already beating on our mother and who would've eventually started beating you.

I understand that you were hurt and confused. I've never talked about it, but I was hurt too. The look on your face when it happened has haunted me for a long time. As bad as he was, and he was bad, he was your father, and the hurt I saw on your face hurt me.

But you showed no concern for me, man. I'm your big brother. I've spent the last sixteen years of my life in prison because your testimony turned voluntary manslaughter into second degree murder. You let Mama put that b.s. in your head, man. We weren't on good terms to begin with. After that, she hated me. And she used you to get even, so to speak.

Anyway, you've written me many letters over the years. You've told me how sorry you are that things turned out the way they did on numerous occasions. So often those words have disgusted me, because how can "I'm sorry" make up for the sixteen years and counting I've lost? They can't!

But I know I gotta forgive you. I don't know how, or how long it will take. But I will. Eventually.

Earnest

CHAPTER 8

"Come here, lil man," JG said proudly, picking up his son and throwing him up into the air a few times. This never failed to bring a smile and laughter out of J Jr. "Damn, he getting big," he said, sitting down with his son, a little winded.

"Jeremy don't be talking like that around him," Jessica said with a slight frown.

"Yeah, boy! You know better than that!" Tina chimed in. "And of course he's getting bigger. That's what people do. We grow! At least, most of us do," she said with a sly smile. Looking away but cutting her eyes at JG.

"Shut up, wench!" JG countered, playfully. "And stop tripping, Jessica. 'Damn' is in the Bible."

"How would you know? You don't even read the Bible," Tina chimed in again.

"So! I know it's in there," he concluded. "Anyway, y'all must have took off early this morning?"

"About four, four-thirty. I knew if we got here early, we could have a good visit and still get back before dark," Jessica stated, matter-of-factly.

"That's what's up. I know y'all gotta be hungry after that long ride. And if you ain't, I am. They fed us some bull…" he stopped short, correcting himself before either of the two women could do it for him. "They fed us some bonafide garbage this morning."

"Boy, you a fool!" Tina said, smiling and shaking her head.

"Now, I know it says something about calling people fools in the Bible!" he declared.

"Yeah, it does. And when you can tell me where it is, I'll apologize."

"Hypocrite!" he jokingly said, standing up. "Come on, Jessica, let's get something to eat. Tina looks uncomfortable without something in her mouth."

"Nig—" This time she had to catch herself.

"That's right. Watch your language around my son," he said, laughing and playfully sticking his tongue out at her as he escorted Jessica to the vending machine.

As they waited in line to get to the hot wings, Jessica couldn't help but to be discouraged. It was obvious to anyone with halfway decent vision that she was in love with JG. But what was even more apparent was his inability or unwillingness to return such love. So, although she would've driven another four hours to make sure her son could spend time with his father on a regular basis, all these visits ever did for her personally was play with her emotions.

"Did you get to take care of that business? I had to put the phone up, so I couldn't call back," he whispered.

"Jeremy, can we ever just enjoy the visit for once?" She was trying not to show how annoyed she was.

"Stop trippin, girl. You know I like to take care of the business first."

"What a shame."

"What a shame? Man, what are you talking about!" He had to catch himself. He was getting loud. "Look," he whispered, "did you take care of the business or what?"

"No, Jeremy, I didn't. And you don't have to worry about me ever doing it again," she said calmly. He nudged her over to the big window looking out over the yard to get what little privacy they could.

"Man, what's wrong with you?" He was visibly upset now. "You ain't had a job in months, Jessica. The business has been feeding you.

And ain't no way in hell my son is going without cause you out there playing."

She turned to face him, holding back tears. "'Playing,' Jeremy. That's what you think; that I'm out there playing? I'm out there raising our son, Jeremy. Alone." She laughed, wiping a tear away. "Man, I don't know why I love you, but I do. I wish I didn't. Because it's eating away at my soul like cancer. And it's becoming clearer each day that you don't love me, and you never will. It hurts, but I'm a big girl. I can deal with it."

"Man, what are you talking about?" he said, frustrated by her newly discovered ability to say no to him. "You know—"

She cut him off. "Please let me finish. Because you're about to come with that same old game claiming that you love me, saying that you love J Jr. I'm alright, I already know where we stand. But if you really love your son so much, why are you here? And don't get me wrong, I'm a realist. I understand we all make mistakes, especially in our younger years, and some cost more than others. But instead of you doing what you need to do to get back home to your son, you're still doing what got you here and what will only keep you here longer than necessary." She was hitting him hard.

"And don't worry about our son going without. He's straight. God has never failed to take care of His business," she smiled, victoriously. "You know, you never asked me how I was doing or anything. But I'll fill you in. I finally passed the NET and Trish got me on at the hospital. I start Monday. So, your son doesn't need your financial support, Jeremy. He needs you," she said, ending the discussion.

JG spent the next three hours holding his son, joking with Tina, and eating. Afterwards, he said his goodbyes. The hardest part of any visit was the end of it, watching your loved ones go in one direction while you went in another. Walking back to the unit, he ran into various business acquaintances.

"Gizzle, what it do?"

"You good, homie?"

"What's happening, J?"

"Is everything everything, bruh?"

"Nah," he answered to all, realizing for the first time ever that not one of them had asked if he'd enjoyed his visit or how his family was doing.

Back in the pod, he ran into Boss going up the stairs. "What's going on, youngster? How your future wife and the lil one doing?" Boss inquired.

"I guess they're straight," he answered somberly, walking on.

"Hold on, J. You guess? Didn't you just come from visit, lil bruh?"

"Yeah, man. But now I almost wish I hadn't gone at all."

"That sounds serious, man. Step into my office," he said, escorting JG into his cell. After they had taken a seat he asked, "So what's going on, man?"

"You ain't gone understand Boss."

"Try me," he patiently replied.

"It's Jessica man, she tripping. Talking bout she ain't gon handle my business no more. Saying I don't love her or my son. Just crazy stuff, man."

"Is she right?" Boss asked straightforwardly.

"Nah, she ain't right! Now you tripping! I talk to you about them all the time, you should know better big bruh." JG explained, hurt by the insinuation.

"Nah, lil bruh. They should know better. And if not, that's a problem," he answered matter-of-factly.

He thought about it and calmed down a little. "Yeah, I guess you're right. But it ain't no way she don't know. I'll do anything for them."

"Look J, I don't get in your business or nothing. You do what you do, and it has nothing to do with me. But how can you expect that girl to know you love her, or your son, if we gon keep it all the way real, when you're willing to jeopardize both of their best interest in the name of a few dollars and a good high?"

"Man, big homie, you sho know how to lift a brother's spirit up when he down," he said with a bitter grin on his face.

"Man, you just got a chance to hug and kiss your family. If that didn't lift your spirits, ain't nothing I can do to help but pray."

"Alright, Bossman," he said surrendering to the truth. "You're right, bruh. I guess I've been looking at it from the wrong perspective."

"You know, J, I really hope you wake up. Man, this game you enjoy playing so much is so wicked that it'll take you away from everything you love. And in certain instances, it'll take everything you love away from you." Boss made the statement looking off into a time he deeply regretted. Feeling the heaviness of the words in the moment, JG decided to leave Boss to himself.

"Man, I appreciate you for always keeping it 100 with me, Boss. I'm bout to kick back for a minute."

"Don't worry about it, J. If I couldn't share my life experiences to keep lil brothers like you from going through it, then everything I went through would have been in vain."

✝

The following morning, while walking back to the pod after a very competitive game of basketball in the gym, JG and Silence were chopping it up.

"Man, I don't know how I missed that last shot," Silence commented, more than a little disappointed in his performance today.

"You don't know how?" questioned JG. "Bruh, you old! You didn't get nothing but an inch off the ground! I should've just blocked it!"

"Old? Lil bruh, I'll do you one on one," he shot back with calm confidence.

"Yeah, you probably would but not until you soak your feet for a couple of days first!" JG said, with a huge smile on his face.

Walking through the front door of the unit, Silence couldn't help but laugh. He didn't just joke like this with many. Some people just didn't know when enough is enough. But JG was cool. Being around him reminded him of the relationship he and his brother once had.

Entering the pod, JG asked, "So what's up, big bruh? Your girl coming today?"

"Nah, my lil brother coming up," he said apprehensively.

"Your lil brother?" JG said this as if it was a fresh revelation from God.

"Yeah, man. We haven't been on the same page for a while. He used to be my dude. He really the only family I got, so…"

"That's what's up, big bruh," he commented, thinking about his own situation.

"Well, I gotta get in that water, homie. Jerome should be here soon."

CHAPTER 9

"So, what is it looking like?" Boss asked.

"Well, I've finished the petition. I brought you a copy to look over before I file it with the court clerk. The law is definitely on our side and the argument is solid. I hope—"

"Excuse me, Mr. Pressi," Boss said, cutting him off. "This is our first time meeting face-to-face but I'm sure my wife has told you all about me. I've been dealing with the law and attorneys and prosecutors and judges and everything else the justice system can throw at you for a long time now. I know how this works, so give it to me straight. Okay?"

"Okay," he responded, appearing to be more relaxed. "Well, you already know how Judge Washburn is. As solid as our argument is, it's unlikely she'll overturn her own ruling."

"That's expected."

"We'll take it to the Court of Criminal Appeals. They recently ruled favorably in a case very similar to yours."

"Blackwell. Yeah, I read that."

"Right," Mr.Pressi said, impressed. "Anyway, the only real difference is the media attention your case received, which is a problem. A lot of people up for re-election." He sounded disgusted.

"Yeah, I know. They made it sound like a wild west shoot out with the Texas Rangers when they actually kicked my door in, unannounced like some robbers." He let out an exasperated chuckle. "Man, I'm by no means absolving myself, but the law is the law. Why won't they just stick to the law?" He sounded wearied by the fight.

"Yeah," Pressi muttered, unsure what to say. "Just hold on. We're fighting and we're going to keep fighting" he said, trying to encourage Boss.

Pressi had sought a law degree because he felt it was a way for him to make a real difference in the world. After graduating from law school and passing the bar, he'd joined the D.A's office expecting to be used as a tool for seeking justice. Instead, he saw the corruption and politics that defines and defiles the judicial system. He saw far too many men and women cornered into taking plea agreements for crimes they were either innocent of or overcharged with from the beginning. After two years on the job, he left to start his own practice in criminal defense. Now he was one of the most sought-after appellate attorneys in the state. Whether he won or lost a case, all his clients knew he had given an honest effort every time because he cared, a quality most attorneys could not genuinely profess.

"Your wife dropped by the office Tuesday and made the final payment. She also asked me to give you this before I left." He passed Boss a white envelope. Boss thanked him, shook his hand, and went back to his cell.

Sitting on the bunk, he ripped open the envelope. Inside was a short, handwritten note from Ebony. It read:

Husband,

I hope you know how much I love you. The time our Lord has blessed us with has been so fulfilling and rewarding for me. You have been as good of a man as any woman could ever hope for. Your faith has encouraged me, your strength has empowered me, and your wisdom has enriched me. I know this fight has wearied you, but don't believe for one second that you are not strong enough to endure it. I know that you are strong enough because I know WHO you depend on for strength.

"Hast thou not known? Hast thou not heard, that the everlasting God, the Lord, the Creator of the ends of the earth fainteth not, neither is weary? There is no searching of his understanding. He giveth power to the faint and to them that have no might he increaseth strength. Even the youths shall faint and be weary, and the young man shall utterly fall: But they that wait upon the Lord shall renew their strength: they shall mount up with wings as eagles; they shall run and not be weary; and they shall walk, and not faint."

Isaiah 40:28-31 KJV

L

Boss just smiled, and once again thanked God for blessing him with this amazing woman. He picked up his CD walkmen, put his earbuds in and pressed play. He already knew what was in it, Marvin Sapp's "Never Would've Made It." He laid down, closed his eyes, and was just about to drift off into a peaceful sleep.

However, his tranquility was interrupted by a knock on the door. He wanted to wave off whoever it was, which would have been justified. You just didn't disturb a man who was trying to sleep. But God had given him a calling in which he was obligated to bear other's burdens, so he got up and opened the door.

"What's going on lil bruh?" It was Lil D, which was a real surprise to Boss. For whatever reason, most of the time he acted as if he was terrified of Boss. But whatever he wanted must be serious. He looked close to tears.

"Uh ... Can I, uh... talk to you for a minute, Boss? I won't take up much of your time, man," he said nervously.

"Yeah, man. Come on in. What's on your mind?"

"Man, I hate to disturb you like this. I know you don't really fool with me, but I really need to talk. I—"

"Hold on, man," Boss interrupted. "Why do you think I don't 'fool 'with you?"

"I don't know, man. That's just the vibe I get."

"Well, don't let your feelings lead you into any misconceptions about me. I don't know you well enough to fool with you or not fool with you. You feel me?" Boss asked, grinning.

"Yeah, I feel you, big bruh."

"So? What's on your mind?"

"Well, today is my father's birthday. He turned fifty-seven. I want to call and wish him a happy birthday so bad, but I can't."

"Why not?"

"It's a long story."

"Look lil bruh, you came over here to talk, so talk."

"Alright. Well, I messed up and got out there on that powder. I hid it from my family, but then I got in the hole. I couldn't pay my debt. My pops owned an auto parts store. He had worked all his life to build his own business." He stopped. You could tell he was hurt. His story is so similar to many others in prison. One bad decision led to another, until they eventually led to one colossal screw up.

"I was desperate," he continued, "the dude I owed was threatening to expose everything to my pops. I couldn't let that happen."

His facial expression was that of a child who was afraid or ashamed of doing something his father would find out about. It's amazing how men well into their twenties, and later, have personality complexes and insecurities as far as their fathers are concerned.

"So," he pressed on, "I robbed his business and burned it down trying to cover it up. Stupid!" He dropped his head like he was living that moment all over again. "We haven't spoken since, and I really don't know what to say."

"Are you remorseful about it?" Boss asked.

"Not a day goes by that I don't regret it, and not because I'm in prison. It's killing me to know that I hurt him like that." The tears were rolling now.

"You obviously love him."

"More than he knows."

Boss put his hand on his shoulder and looked him dead in the face. "That's what you tell him lil brother."

"It ain't that easy, man!"

"It never is. But it's a lot easier than dealing with the fact that you never took the opportunity to say it when you could." He finally lifted up his head and looked at Boss.

"Man," Boss resumed, "relationships have been irreparably damaged by closed mouths. We refuse to say what needs to be said, either out of fear or pride. Both of which can not only destroy relationships but can also destroy people."

"Yeah."

Lil D stood up, resolved to call his pops, come what may. He had lived with this fear and insecurity long enough. It was time to do something about it before it destroyed him.

"Thanks man. I really appreciate you listening to me."

"No problem, man. Anytime. I fool with you," Boss said, smiling. Lil D smiled back at him.

"Lil bruh, do you mind if I pray with you before you leave?"

"Nah, man. I need it."

Marcus was sitting in the library reading a book. He often came here to get away from the distractions of the pod. In an environment as small and chaotic as prison is, any man who hopes to hold onto his sanity must search out a temporary haven or create one. Yet even those moments of peace are often interrupted.

"What's good, MJ?"

Recognizing JG's voice, he looked up from his book. "J Money, what's up with you?" He paused, as if a surprising thought had just hit him. "Man, what are you doing in the library?"

"Well, you know me, always looking for something new to get off into," he said, throwing a casual, confident glance at the young female CO sitting behind the desk in the office. Sitting down next to Marcus, he pointed at the book on the table.

"*The Outrageous Love of God*, what's that about?" he asked.

"You ever heard of the Prodigal Son?"

"Yeah, a little bit. Is that what it's about?"

"Kinda. To me it's about second chances, how God doesn't give up on us no matter how far we stray away. How He's always ready for us to come back home. How valuable we are to God. All that."

"Man, you really believe that?"

"I don't know. I want to," Marcus responded. "Do you?"

"It don't really matter man. You can believe whatever you want. But the only thing that we can deal with is reality."

"Reality! Man, the way you run around here you act like you ain't even in prison."

"It may look like that on the outside looking in, but I know exactly where I'm at. And trust me, I got as many problems as the next man. I just deal with it in my own way."

"And what way is that?" Marcus asked, expecting to receive some privileged information.

JG leaned in as if he was about to share something deep, and then he slowly whispered, "I stay high. I chase women and hustle. I throw money at my problems. And if that don't work, I smoke some more."

"Yeah, but they're still there when you come down off your high!"

"That's why I stay high! Man, you ain't paying attention?" he said, smiling.

"You wild, man," Marcus responded, shaking his head and laughing.

"Man, I'm just doing what gets me by until these gates open up for me. I don't really think about God and all of that. If God loves us so much, and if we're so valuable to Him, why does He let us go through so much hell down here?"

"I don't know. But I was in the same car, in the same wreck that killed my brother. It could've easily killed me. But I'm still here. I find it hard to believe that the only purpose in all this is to torment me and my family. So, I'm seeking answers."

"That's cool. Keep seeking lil bruh. I hope you find what you're looking for," JG said. "But ol girl been checking me out since I stepped through the door, so I'm about to go seek to have an unauthorized relationship. You feel me?" he whispered and walked off.

CHAPTER 10

In prison it's a must that you learn how to "jail" quickly. Figuring out how to live compatibly in the cell with another personality is a huge step in the process, because you spend so much of your time in the cell. Especially during count time, and those dreaded lockdowns due to violence and shakedowns. Normally, because they share so many interests, Silence and Marcus get along wonderfully. They passed the time talking about life, education, and God, and a highly competitive game of chess or Scrabble was always one challenge away.

However, Silence had been in a zone of his own since the visit with his brother. There were always days when he would be working on some projects or days where he would be "locked in" until he completed it, but lately, his busyness appeared to be more like a mask or force-field, or in Silence's case, a 'Beware of Dog' sign. This was a boundary Marcus had learned from experience not to cross, but he needed to talk. Silence had become like a big brother to him.

So, with the confidence of a beloved little brother, Marcus hopped off the top bunk, walked to the door, and glanced out of the window. Sighing, he turned around and looked at Silence sitting at the desk before sheepishly asking, "Hey, big bruh, you busy?"

Slipping his headphones off and looking up from his schoolwork, Silence responded, "What?" with a look of annoyance.

"Um. I mean, um, are you still busy, big bruh?" he asked again, confidence teetering.

"What does it look like, bruh?" he shot back, clearly agitated.

"That's what's up," Marcus said, climbing back up on the top bunk, noticeably hurt by the rebuffing.

Ever aware of his actions, Silence let out a sigh of his own and said, "My bad, lil bruh. I shouldn't have snapped at you like that. What's up, man? What's on your mind?" he asked.

"Nah, it's cool, bruh." Marcus wouldn't look at him. He just lay there flipping through the channels on his television.

"Come on, homie. Don't start acting like a little girl," Silence said, needling him.

"Man, I ain't on that."

"Well, what's up? You obviously wanted to rap. You need me to show you how to come up on that lil nurse you been stalking?"

"Man, you tripping! I don't stalk them, they stalk me!" Marcus exclaimed.

"So, if it ain't that, what is it?" he asked, seeing that they had gotten past the earlier offense.

"I'm good, big bruh. For real. I was worried about you."

"Why is that?"

"You ain't been yourself since you came back from visit, bruh."

"Man, you know my story. Since I've been in here it's just been me and the occasional female that was willing to ride with me for a season. And I was cool with that. I had grown accustomed to it. It made life less complicated. Less emotions involved. So, seeing Jerome got to me a lil bit. I felt things I haven't felt in a long time." He said this with a nostalgic look on his face. "Man, we were tight. That was my dude. After everything that went down, I was crushed. I wanted to hate him. I actually thought I did. But once I saw him, I knew I never did. Never could. I was just hurt, man."

"Did you tell him that?"

"Yeah. And he felt me. He always knew. But do you know what he said?"

"What?"

"He said he was hurt too." Silence said this with a flabbergasted chuckle. Marcus didn't say a word. He just waited.

"Yeah, he was hurt. He said he had always looked up to me. He saw my focus and drive. In his eyes, nothing could stop me from accomplishing whatever I desired." He had a faraway look in his eyes again. "He knew I had to be hustling but, no matter what people said about me, he refused to believe I would take someone's life unless it was absolutely necessary."

He paused and Marcus waited.

"You know, I had always told myself that I had to do it. That I didn't have a choice. But as we talked, I realized I was lying to myself. In my heart I knew it." He paused yet again, reflecting.

"He was sloppy drunk. I had beaten him down and taken the knife from him. All I had to do was walk away. Instead, I chose to kill him. In front of his wife and son. There was no way he could look up to me after that. He lost his dad and his hero at the same time."

The two of them sat there quietly for a few minutes. Each undoubtedly pondering how so many lives can be altered so drastically by a decision made by one individual. Both of their families were crippled, and the weight of it rested squarely on their shoulders.

"So," Silence asked, "does that answer your question?"

Laying on the top bunk staring at the ceiling, Marcus quietly responded, "Yeah," and went off into a zone of his own.

What's up, Pops? Happy belated birthday! I hope you enjoyed yourself. I've been meaning to write you for a while now, but I really didn't know what to say. I didn't think you wanted to hear anything I had to say anyway. But I talked to a brother in here who reminds me a lot of you, and he gave me some helpful advice.

I know I messed up, Pops! I live with it every day. And it is not because I'm locked up. I can deal with that. What haunts me is the fact that it hurt you. I've looked up to you all my life, and all I've ever desired to do is make you proud. But all I ever seemed to do was disappoint you. So, when I got myself in debt, I figured I couldn't bring it to you, so I tried to handle it myself. I never imagined it would turn out the way it did.

I know nothing I can say or do will make up for what I've done to you and our family. But as momma always says: I pray that you can find it in your heart to forgive me. I love you, Pops. I always will.

Truly,
Your Son
Detrick

†

"What's up, bay-bee!" Boss exclaimed, wrapping Ebony in his arms.

"Hey, baby," She responded, looking up into his eyes and giving him a kiss. "You want anything to eat or drink?" she asked, gesturing toward the row of vending machines.

"Not right now. I just want to sit down and hold my wife for a while."

They found a couple of seats next to the big windows overlooking the parking lot. They sat back and Boss threw his massive arm over the back of Ebony's seat. She laid her head on his arm and closed her eyes.

"So, how are you feeling, baby?" Boss inquired.

"I'm good," she responded, eyes still closed.

"Look at me, baby." His voice was concerned and commanding.

"What's wrong, Otis?"

"You tell me."

She leaned forward and laughed, "Man, I knew that big-mouthed sister of mine was going to say something."

"And that's why I love her. Now, what's going on?"

"It's nothing, baby. I got dizzy at work the other day and went to the doctor just to be on the safe side. My blood pressure was up a little. That's all!"

"And why didn't you feel the need to tell me about it?"

"Because I didn't want you worrying for nothing."

"For nothing! Baby!" Boss was incredulous. "First of all, nothing that involves you is 'nothing' to me. Period! You're my wife. And you know I'm not the type to do a whole lot of worrying. Then we'll both have high blood pressure. I like to know what's going on, so I'll know what to be praying about."

"I know, baby. And I apologize," she said, relenting.

"So, what did the doctor say?" Boss asked, continuing his interrogation.

"Otis, be cool. He ran some tests. The results will be back in a week or so. As soon as I know something, you'll know. Okay, Lieutenant Hamilton?" she said, with a wry smile.

"Captain Hamilton!" he retorted, smiling as well.

They both were laughing now, thankful for one another's presence. For the next five hours they talked about family and faith and played Casino and Rummy when they weren't eating. It was in these moments where they gained the strength to maintain a love that had endured over twenty years of incarceration. As they did at the end of every visit, they held hands, bowed their heads and prayed to the God of all comfort. Even under these circumstances, He's good.

CHAPTER 11

"Hello?" Jessica answered.

"What's up, boo!" JG exclaimed.

"Who is this?"

"What you mean, who is this? It's the 'who' whose son you gave birth to. Don't play with me!" JG said with an irritated tone, not getting the reception he expected.

"Oh, what's up?" Jessica cooly responded. "Why did y'all block out the number? I almost didn't answer."

"You better answer when daddy calls," he piqued in his "Sweat Hotel" voice.

"Yeah, whatever. You're J. Jr's daddy, not mine," she retorted. "Anyway, why didn't you call collect. Why you got Tina doing three ways for you when she is at work?"

"I didn't call from Tina's phone."

"Whose phone did you call from?" she reluctantly asked, knowing the answer.

"Mine."

"Jeremy," she expressed, tiredly, "you said you were done with that when you had to flush the other one to keep from getting caught with it."

"I did," he responded, matter of factly.

"So, what the..." she caught herself. An argument wouldn't accomplish anything "Look Jeremy, I don't wanna participate in anything that could keep you in there any longer than necessary. So, I'm going to ask you not to call me any more from a cell phone."

"What you say?!" He was beside himself.

"You heard me."

"Yeah, I heard you. Now I want you to hear me. I'm gon call my son *however* I want to, *whenever* I want to. *Period!*"

"Okay," she replied, unperturbed. "Your son is asleep at the moment. Would you like me to wake him up *daddy?*" she spat out, sarcastically.

"Nah, that's alright," he said humorously.

"Okay. Goodbye, then," she said, hanging up.

JG sat there staring at the phone for a few seconds, and even considered calling back to straighten her out. But in the end, he decided to roll up and forget about it. He knew what it was anyway. It was that dude she had been fooling around with for a few months now. Ol boy must've been hating on him. But it was cool. He'd be out soon, and Jessica would forget all of this ever happened.

A knock on the door brought him out of his musing. He got up and peeked through the small hole he had poked into the "blind" he had that covered the window. He buzzed the door open by pressing the electronic button on the wall next to the door.

"What's good, Menace?" he asked, sitting back on the bunk.

"Ain't nothing, fool. Trying to see if you still straight?" Menace was tall and skinny, pants hanging to his knees. His long dreads hung over his face, concealing his shifty looking eyes. If they hadn't grown up in the same hood, JG probably wouldn't mess with him like he did because Menace was known to be on shyst. But he and JG had never had any problems before.

"Yeah, I got a few quarters left."

"Nah, homie. I'm just trying to get a thump. I got some chips and coffee, you know."

"You holler at Smooth?"

"Yeah, that fool said he was out."

"Well, I ain't got nothing but a few bags left. But I was getting ready to go up. You wanna smoke?"

"Come on, fool. You know I wanna smoke. That's why I'm over here. But me and the homeboy Loco was gon go in on one."

"Loco? Who is that?"

"He just got here from out west. He straight, J," Menace pleaded half-heartedly, trying to put him at ease.

"Alright. Go get him," JG said, apprehensively.

Menace came back a few minutes later with a short, muscular, brown-skinned dude following him. *He definitely needs to be watched,* JG thought. His eyes were dark and cold, and his every movement looked threatening.

"What it is," he said, looking around the cell as if he was casing it. He sat on the toilet next to the door and Menace sat on the bunk next to JG.

"What's good, bruh? I'm JG." He was starting to feel uneasy.

"I'm Loco, homie. 'Preciate you for showing love like this."

"It ain't nothing," JG said, firing up the blunt he had rolled, taking two long pulls before passing it to Menace.

They smoked the rest of the blunt, making small talk as they did; What prison had Loco come from, what was it like, was such and such still there, etc. etc. etc. When they were finished, Menace stood up and walked toward the door as if they were about to leave. Instead, he posted up with his back to the door. Loco, still sitting on the toilet, asked, "You mind if I make a call, homie?" with a sardonic smile on his face.

JG knew what that meant. They didn't just want to smoke. They wanted to know if he was straight. This was a robbery, and he had foolishly opened himself up to it. Maybe he could talk his way out of it.

"Man, I'm waiting on Sprint to hit me back right now. My card froze up and they talking about turning it off today if I don't give them another method of payment. Once I get that straightened out, I got ya."

"Nah, homie. You got me right now!" Loco spat out, pulling an ice pick-like weapon from his waistband. At the same time Menace was coming out of his pocket with something that looked like an old kitchen butcher knife. JG stood up, holding his hands up in front of him as a sign of surrender.

"Menace?! What's up with this homie?!" he pleaded.

"You know what it is, J. Whatever the homeboy do is cool. Just give him what we want, and we gone."

With lightning quick speed Loco caught JG with a jaw-rattling blow that knocked him back down on the bunk, dazing him.

"Sucka, you must think I'm playing with you!"

JG grabbed the phone and charger from the head of the bunk and handed it to him.

"Nah, fool. Come on with that sack, too!"

JG reached into his pocket, brought out a few bags of weed and gave them to him.

"Come on, J. I know you. If you say you got a few that means you got a couple ounces, at least. Don't make us hurt you, fool," Menace said cooly.

"I told you what I had, man. That's all I got," he cried out.

"Alright. If that's how you wanna play it, that's how we'll play it. But it's gon get ugly in here, J. I got life. This fool here got life. We ain't got nothing to lose, homie," Menace asserted, with little emotion.

JG, though far from a coward, was no fool either. He was not willing to die for something he could replace tomorrow. So, he slowly grabbed his boom box off the desk and pulled a component loose that revealed a secret compartment. Inside was a package the size of a salt shaker, tightly wrapped in black electrical tape. He tossed it to Menace.

"That's all of it man." He was close to tears.

"What's up, Menace," Loco asked. "What you wanna do?"

"I believe him. That's everything. And next time he decides to make a move on this compound, I know he'll be to see us first. Right, J?"

JG didn't say a word. He just sat there shocked, seething, wondering how this had happened and how he was going to deal with it.

"Man, dude still think we playing!" Loco growled out, about to attack. JG stood up to defend himself.

"Nah, homie! Chill out. We got what we came for. Ain't no need to butcher him, fool. But J, if I ever feel like you wanna shake something, you gotta go. You feel me?!"

"Yeah. Ya'll got that, man." And they left.

The unit was on edge after news of the robbery got out. Boss and Silence heard about it as soon as they returned from working out on the big yard. They went straight to JG's cell. Boss was sitting at the desk, silently praying. There was no other way to put it; this was a life-or-death situation. JG could either walk away from the game or take a few steps further into the darkness. If he didn't retaliate, he would never be allowed to hustle again without paying protection fees to one group or another. If he did, it was kill or be killed. And killing usually leads to more killing. The only other option was to square up.

At the moment, he was standing in front of the mirror checking out the damage. Silence was standing at the door, looking out into the pod.

"So, what you wanna do J?" Silence asked, matter-of-factly.

"Come on, Silence?" he asked skeptically. "I appreciate you checking on me, but them dudes your homies, man."

"True. But I fool with you. If I didn't, I'd be over there getting broke off like a big homie should. And making sure you didn't spend another minute on this compound. Period!" Silence turned to look at him. "But I do fool with you. So, I'm asking, how you wanna handle this?"

"Man, what can I do?" he asked, dabbing at the cut under his eye with an alcohol pad. "It's too many of them dudes! I can't fight 'em all!"

Silence almost laughed at the term "them dudes" to describe him and his homies, but he took no offense. He understood where he was coming from.

"If you want to, I can get you a one on one with Menace and Loco. It'll help restore your reputation a little. Show everybody that you're not a coward. But I can't ask them to give you your stuff back. That's gone."

"Yeah," JG sadly whispered, thinking about the phone he had just got.

"But you do realize it's just a matter of time before somebody else tries you. It might not go like this next time. It might take some real bloodshed. You're not guaranteed to walk away from that."

JG let out a big sigh and stared into the mirror. He was almost in tears. How could he let this go and walk around with his head held high? His reputation with the female staff would be permanently damaged.

"Hey E, let me talk to the lil brother for a minute." Boss said.

"Alright, big bruh. I need to go over here and get at these fools anyway," Silence said as he walked out of the door, all eyes on him.

"Come over here and sit down so I can holler at you, lil bruh."

"Boss, you don't understand, man!" Now that they were alone the tears were rolling. His fists were clenched, and he was so angry, he was visibly shaking.

"If you only knew." Boss said heavily heartedly.

"Knew what, Boss! You don't have to deal with this! You don't live that life no more! And if you did, you wouldn't let nobody get away with this!" He was angry and frustrated. He needed to vent. Boss just sat there and let him get it off.

"You got 'death before dishonor' tatted on your arm, man! *Death* before dishonor! Them dudes disrespected me, man! Treated me like a sucka, and I was trying to show love! That's what I know!"

Boss quietly sat there, biding his time. JG just angrily paced the floor, occasionally glancing in the mirror.

"Alright. Are you done now?" Boss asked.

"Look, man! I ain't feeling—"

"I asked if you were done?" Boss interrupted, forcefully. He was determined to get out what he intended to say.

JG had never heard him use that tone before. "Yeah, I'm done, big bruh," he said respectfully.

"Well sit down for a minute and listen to what I have to say. It may help, man."

JG sat down on the end of the bunk with his head down.

"You're right, lil bruh. I've been out of the game for a long time. And thank God for that. When I was your age, I probably would've went kamikaze if somebody had tried me like that. But at your age I didn't feel like I had anything to lose. I had a fresh thirty-five in the state plus a consecutive twenty-five in the feds. And the only person I had in my corner was a woman who I figured would only stick around for a year or two. Five, at best. I had no hope."

Boss had tears welling up in his eyes. "It's only by the grace of God I'm still here, man! But you do have hope. It could've went the other way when you shot dude. He could've shot you first or he could've easily died, but he didn't. You were blessed to end up with the time you did. You have a son, and a woman who loves you more than you deserve, to be honest. You dog her out, and she still makes sure you see your son at least once a month. When I got locked up, as far as my son's mother was concerned, I died. But you got a real family, man!" He said this with what sounded like a personal longing.

"What would you be telling them if you pursued this? That they're not as important to you as your 'rep'? That phones and dope are more valuable to you than your freedom? More valuable than your *life*? Is that really who you are, man?"

JG sat there in deep thought, taking it all in.

✝

A few months had passed since the robbery. JG had taken Boss' advice and let it go. It had cost him a few dollars and a little shame, but it had also gradually given him a sense of peace he hadn't previously known. When you're in "the game" you have to deal with a lot of issues that rob you, figuratively, and sometimes literally, of your peace. There was the pressure to come up with the move. The pressure to deliver the money and drugs on time. The pressure of hiding the dope from the police. The pressure of flipping it quick enough to keep the move from straying, and, of course, defending it from the literal robbers. Pressure on top of pressure. It's a stressful way of life, which often deprives you of rest and relaxation. Despite the rewards, JG was learning to appreciate life without the consequences that came with it. He was on his way downstairs to rap with Silence when he ran into Lil D.

"What's up, D?" he asked.

"What's happening, J? What you got going on?"

"Man, I aint on nothing. Bout to get up with Silence for a minute."

"Ah yeah. You still laying low?" Lil D inquired, doubtfully.

"Nah, man, I ain't laying low. I'm done, bruh!" he said, unsure himself if he could live without the hustle.

"Yeah? That's what's up, then. I need to stop smoking myself. I go up for parole in nine months."

"For real! Now that's what's up! Man, do whatever you gotta do to get out of here! ASAP! This place gon drain the life out of you," he said, with real conviction. "But get up with me later. I'ma slide down here and holler at Silence."

"Alright, J."

JG made his way to Silence's cell and looked in the door window. He saw Marcus sitting at the desk reading, so he knocked on the door. Marcus looked up and waved him in.

"What's going on, JG?" he asked.

"What's good, Lil Marcus? Where your celly at?"

"I don't know. Probably in Boss' cell."

"Yeah, he probably is," JG said, looking at the papers and charts spread across the top bunk. "Man, what you in here working on? A hostile takeover?"

Marcus laughed. "Something like that. I'm revising my business plan."

"What kind of business is it?"

"Cabinet-making. I graduated from the class, so I might as well put what I learned to use."

"Oh yeah. Any money in it?"

"It is. If you can distinguish yourself from the competition. Thus…" Marcus said, pointing at all the papers on his bed.

"I need to start me a business," JG commented, somewhat serious.

"What do you know how to do?"

"Hustle, gamble, and mack." They both laughed.

"You might not believe it, but those are actually good traits to have as an entrepreneur. You just gotta learn how to transition them to the legitimate side of business."

"Oh yeah. How?" JG asked, a little intrigued.

"Well, what kind of things are you interested in?"

"Hustling, gambling, and macking! Man, we already went over this."

"Okay," Marcus said, smiling, "other than the money, what really draws you to hustling?"

"I don't know. I ain't never thought about it," he said, pondering on it. "I guess it's the flip. Turning something small into something big. The grind. The networking. I get a thrill out of it." JG was getting stirred up.

"That's good. What about gambling?"

"Oh, that's easy. The risk. The excitement of winning big, and even losing big, with one roll of the dice. Sometimes you get spanked, but I think it's worth it."

"That's the essence of entrepreneurship. And what about macking?"

"Ah man, we gotta get you outta here, lil bruh," JG said, with a mischievous smile.

Marcus finally caught on to the joke. "Man, stop playing! I'm for real. You silly, bruh!"

"My bad, homie," he said, still laughing. "For real, though. This might sound messed up, but I like being able to talk somebody into doing what I want them to do even when they really don't want to do it," he said, matter-of-factly.

"Yeah, that does sound messed up. You might need some professional help. But it's a good resource to possess in the business world. All of them are," Marcus replied, deep in thought.

"I tell you what; let's get up some more and see if we can come up with a plan for you. Once we figure out the options it'll be easier. I'm no 'expert' but I believe I can help you put a business plan together, if you're serious."

"That's what's up," JG said, mind now racing.

Later that day JG and Lil D we're sitting in Lil D's cell smoking a blunt.

"Man, who you get this from?" JG asked, passing the blunt to Lil D with a look of dissatisfaction.

"Smooth," Lil D responded, unfazed by his friend's grumbling.

"Did you pay for it?" JG jokingly asked.

"Man, whatever. You ain't stopped hitting it!" he said, passing the blunt to JG.

"I'm hoping if I hit it enough times, I might feel something!"

"Man, give me my weed!" Lil D reached for the blunt, but JG held him off with his forearm.

"Stop playing fool!" he said laughing. "You trying to blow what lil high I got!"

They finished smoking and kicked back to watch a basketball game on tv.

"Hey D, I know your people own businesses and stuff. You know anything about running one?"

"Why'd you ask me that?" Lil D was surprised.

"Well, I was talking to Silence's celly, Marcus, today, and he was messing around with business plans and stuff like that. The youngster got a real head on his shoulders. Anyway, I'm supposed to be getting up with him about putting a business plan together."

"What kind of business you gon run," Lil D asked, somewhat skeptically.

"Why you gotta say it like that, fool? You don't think I can run a business?"

"Nah, that ain't what I'm saying, man. It's just surprising to hear you talking like that. Anyway, what kind of business are you thinking about?"

"I don't know. Maybe a casino or a massage parlor?"

"Come on, man," Lil D responded with a deadpan face. "If you gon do it, take it seriously."

"What you mean?" JG said, feeling a little disrespected. "I am serious. Those are legitimate businesses."

"Yeah, but how you gon raise enough legitimate money to open a casino. Plus, you need some political connections that people like us don't have. You feel me?"

"Yeah, I guess you're right."

"And if you open a massage parlor you might as well start pimping," he said, laughing. JG laughed as well. That *was* funny.

"Alright, Jay Z. What kind of business would you open?" he asked sarcastically.

"I'm gon open a detail shop," he said with confidence.

"Oh, you *been* thinking about owning a business?"

"Yeah," he said, shrugging his shoulders. "Bruh, I was the black sheep, but I paid attention. I saw my Pops in action. The late nights, hours and hours of planning, day after day, for years. I didn't do anything with it out there, but when I got locked up, I had a lot of time on my hands."

"Man, every time I see you, you either getting high or trying to get high!" JG exclaimed.

"True. And when I get high, I think a lot."

"Man, I really been wasting time. The dude I been serving since he came to prison is further ahead than I am."

Lil D just shrugged the comment off with no offense taken. He was used to JG's sense of humor. "I ain't got it all together J, but I know that if I'm not planning on what I can do to stay out of here, by default I'm planning on what I can do to come back."

CHAPTER 12

L il D was walking past Boss' cell as he was stepping out of the door. "What's up, Lil D?" he asked with a smile.

"Oh, what's going on, Boss? You take the day off?"

"Yeah. I didn't feel like dealing with that kitchen today."

"Man, I've always wondered why you didn't work in the library or the chapel? You seem like you're better suited for that."

"Probably so. But I worked in the library for a few years. It can drain you, mentally and emotionally. Dealing with that crooked justice system on a daily basis. Nah. I'ma let the Lord and my lawyer bear that burden."

"So why don't you go to the chapel? You can do a lot of good down there."

"Yeah. But I can do a lot *more* good if I focus on bringing the chapel *here*." You could tell he was passionate about this.

"Yeah. I guess you're right." Lil D was impressed. He was always so genuine.

"So, how did it go with your pops?" Boss inquired.

"I didn't have the nerves to call, but I wrote him. My mama said she gave him the letter. I ain't heard nothing from him. It is what it is, you know." You could tell it hurt.

"Man, just keep praying. If you know the God I know, He'll work it out," Boss said confidently.

"How do you know that, big bruh?" Lil D asked, seriously. "I went to church and prayed before I went to trial, but God didn't work that out."

"He didn't?"

"Nah! I'm in prison."

"Oh, your idea of God 'working it out' is giving you whatever you ask for. Is that how you see it?"

"Nah, but…" He was at a loss.

"But what? You probably weren't thinking about God before you got arrested."

"I went to church almost every week."

"There are people who 'go to church' two or three times *every* week and aren't truly thinking about God. They go because they were raised in a household that went to church. They go because the culture dictates that you go to church. They go to meet women or men. But going to express their love and adoration for who God is, and what He has done in giving his Son that we could be reconciled with Him, is the furthest thing from their minds. Not to mention that many of them don't take sin seriously. And if you don't take sin seriously, you can't take God seriously."

"Why do you say that?"

"Because God hates sin, lil bruh. Sin is offensive to God. It started in the garden with Adam and Eve's disobedience, and ever since then, man has existed with a heart of rebellion toward God. That rebellion separates us from God. And apart from God, we live in a manner that is harmful to us and others."

"Alright. I guess I get where you're coming from. But what does that have to do with my original question?"

"You have no idea where I'm coming from, lil bruh, because it has everything to do with your original question," Boss replied, pausing for a second before continuing. "I said, 'if you know the God I know, He'll work it out.' You asked, 'How do I know that?' Well, the God *I know* works all things out for my good. When I say I know Him, I mean I know Him for who He truly is, the Sovereign God of the universe. I know Him as the only answer to my sin problem, my Redeemer. And I know Him as my Provider, the One who works things out on my behalf. I know this from experience. And if you know Him as I do, the same is true for you."

"What if I don't know Him like that?" Lil D questioned.

"Then, in my estimate, you don't know Him at all. You only know of Him."

"What's the difference?"

"I know my wife. I know everything there is to know about her. We have spent so many intimate moments, shared so many experiences, that I can genuinely say I know her. I know what she will and will not do. I know how she responds to certain situations. I know how she thinks and processes things. We talk every day, and though she is not with me physically, we share a spiritual and emotional bond that is just as real. Just as tangible. Anita Baker, on the other hand, is someone I only know of. I listen to and enjoy her music regularly. But I know nothing about her personally because we have not shared any experiences. Similarly, God does not just want us to hear about Him from others, He wants us to experience Him personally. Then, and only then, will you know how real He is. Then you'll be able to know that no matter what it looks like, God is working it out for your good."

Lil D looked at Boss as if it was for the first time. He had always admired him, and knew he was a different breed. But now he knew why. He had *faith*. Real faith. Passionate, unshakable faith. Faith which allowed him to see life where others saw death and be light in a place overrun by darkness. And in that moment, he was convinced that God was real. He'd seen others profess it, but from day one Boss had been the portrait of God's life-transforming power.

"Man, I wanna know God like that. I need to," he said, looking at Boss with tears in his eyes.

Boss let out a deep sigh of relief and nodded his head in approval. There were tears in his eyes as well. He placed his hand on the younger man's shoulder and led him in prayer as they bowed their heads. After they had finished, Boss said. "Whether you realize it or not, He did answer the prayer you prayed before you went to trial, He worked it out for you. Just not how you expected," leaving Lil D with something else to think about.

✝

Lil D had been thinking a lot about what he'd experienced the other day. He knew something special and life-transforming had taken place, but he didn't know how he should feel or what to do about it. He'd wanted to go and talk to Boss some more, but he felt like a hypocrite because he was still getting high. For that reason, he had actually been dodging him. Boss had taken the initiative and come to check on him a few times, but he always made himself elusive. Right now, he was getting ready to duck off in the corner of the library behind a row of bookshelves to find some solitude. To his surprise, Silence came out of the restroom and spotted him. They weren't close friends or anything, but since they had lived in the same pod for a couple of years now, they were well- acquainted with one another. Silence grabbed some papers from the front desk and came to join him.

"What's going on, D?" he said, sitting down.

"Not too much, man. I just felt like getting away from the pod. My celly didn't have to work today, so I decided to get out of his way for a while."

"Yeah," Silence replied, somewhat distracted by the papers in front of him.

"What you got going on?" Lil D inquired.

"Man, filling out these parole papers. Then I got some recommendations for my supervisor and counselor to sign." He sounded skeptical.

"It seems like you're worried about it, but I don't know why. If anybody's ready, it's you."

Silence laughed. "Man, if being ready was the only requirement, I would've made parole five years ago."

"What you mean?" Lil D asked, considering his own parole hearing that was coming up.

"Lil bruh, I've seen dudes go up there with college degrees, every certificate you can get in prison, family support, a job waiting on em, and write-up free. Denied!" he said dramatically. "Then I've seen dudes go up there with nothing speaking on their behalf *but* write-ups, and they let them go," he finished, shaking his head with a dumbfounded look on his face.

"So, what you suppose to do?" Lil D asked with concern.

"Time and chance is my philosophy."

"What?"

"Ecclesiastes 9:11. Sometimes, no matter how well you plan your life, it all comes down to time and chance. So, when your time comes, be prepared to take advantage of the chance you've been given."

"So... no matter how prepared you might be, if it ain't your time, it just ain't your time."

"I don't know if that's what Solomon meant, but that's my take."

"That ain't straight!"

"I agree. But as far as I can tell, that's life."

"So, you might as well just do you?" Lil D said, discouraged.

"Nah, man. That's not the point. You still need to be prepared to take advantage of your chance when it comes. A lot of them dudes who got out of here unprepared are back with more time. Some are just existing out there; not actually living. Some got killed in them streets. If I would've made parole five years ago that might've been me. Who knows? Right now, I'm better prepared to take advantage of my chance, but if it ain't my time it ain't my time."

"Man, how is it that the parole board gets to decide when it's your time, or mine?"

"They're not."

"Well, who are you..." Lil D stopped short. "Oh! You're talking about God," he said, curiously.

"Yeah. Does that surprise you?" He asked, noticing the hint of astonishment in his voice.

"Not surprised, really. I just didn't know you were into religion like that."

"I'm not 'into religion like that.' I'm into life. And you can't begin to talk about life unless you start from the beginning."

"You sound like Boss," Lil D observed.

"Well," Silence responded understandingly, "that's my guy. We disagree on some things, but we both believe in God, or a higher power, or the universe, something. He's always shooting some stuff at me. I'm still looking into it."

"You mean about Jesus?"

"I suppose," he said smiling. "At least that's where he's at. I don't know. I'm searching, though. I've been fed so much from so many sources that I'm still sifting through it to find out what's real and what isn't. But when I look at Boss' lifestyle, it makes a real good case for Jesus. He's genuine. But I know dudes with other beliefs who are just as genuine. Who am I to say who's right and who's wrong."

"Yeah," Lil D responded, wishing he was more confident in the profession he had made days earlier.

A couple of weeks later Lil D was lying in bed reading *Kairo! The Journey of an Urban Pilgrim* by Judah Ben, when the officer slid some mail under the door. He sat up and walked over to pick it up. It was a letter from his dad. He sat back down and stared at the letter in his hand. His eyes started to water before he even opened it. He had no idea what the contents of the letter were; he was simply happy to hear from the man he'd looked up to his entire life.

He finally opened the envelope, and the first thing he noticed was a picture of his father. He took it out of the envelope and stared intently at an image of who he would be twenty-five years from now. *If I'm lucky*, he thought. His pops had aged well. And he still had a fire for life in his eyes. Setting the picture down on the bed next to him, he unfolded the letter.

Son,

I'm not good at this. I haven't written a letter since I was in school, trying to convince your mother that she didn't want to miss out on a good thing. Thank God it worked, because I didn't have any more game, as you kids call it. She didn't go for what I thought was game, anyhow. She saw something in me that I couldn't even see. And Detrick, I want you to know I see those same things in you. Even better things. But it's not enough for me to see it; you have to see it!

I was never angry with you for burning down my store, I was disappointed in you for burning down your store. For destroying your life. I was hurt because you thought so little of yourself that you could throw your life away so easily. I know I didn't make it any better, always finding fault in you. And I apologize. But son, when no one else believes in you, believe in yourself. I asked your mother and sister to promise not to tell you, but it's time I did. I have prostate cancer.

I'm having surgery in two weeks, but it doesn't look good. and I refuse to take your mother through what chemo will do to me, so you're the "man of the house "now. Be strong and of good courage, son. And always remember that I believe in you. And I love you.

You

Detrick was sitting on the edge of the bunk gripping the letter with both hands. He was rocking back and forth as tears streamed down his face. He had never been as proud as he was to be his father's son as he was right then. And he had never been as sad. With these emotions waging war within him, he dropped the letter on the floor, fell back on the bunk, and wept.

CHAPTER 13

Silence was watching the game and eating a burrito when Marcus walked into the cell.

"What's the score?" he asked, reaching for a burrito of his own from the bowl on the desk. "Man, you know we handling that," Silence smugly stated.

"Alright, but what's the score?"

"We're up by six with almost four minutes to go."

"Handling that?" Marcus said sarcastically. "Man, y'all ain't handling nothing, and we got the ball!" he excitedly said as the game came back on from commercial break.

"That means nothing, lil bruh," he replied, pointing at the tv screen. "Y'all ain't moved the ball past the fifty all second half. Don't play!"

As he was talking, the defensive back intercepted the pass from the quarterback and ran into the endzone untouched. Silence sat back on the bed as if he was never worried. Marcus dropped his head in disgust and sat down next to him.

"Where have you been at, anyway? I can't believe you missed *this* game."

"I been in JG's cell working on business plans with him and Lil D."

"Yeah. How is D doing?" Silence asked with concern.

"Better. It's been a little while now, so I guess the sting has worn off. I know he's focused. He stopped getting high and everything."

"That figures. He really loved his pops."

"Yeah," Marcus said, changing the subject. "But JG was a real surprise. He's been hunting me down to talk about any and everything business related."

"He's a hustla. That's what hustlas do. You turned him on to something new, and he in grind mode."

A less entertaining game followed their rivalry game. Marcus hopped up on the bunk to relax a little. His mind was consumed by his recent discussion with JG and Lil D. Of them all, he was the youngest, but by far the most knowledgeable when it came to business. At least in theory. Yet the other two men had a drive about them that made him more sure of their success than he was of his own.

A couple of days later Marcus was in Boss' cell returning a book. He was sitting on the floor by the door sifting through a pile of books that Boss kept in a bag hanging on the wall.

"So, what did you think about the book?" Boss inquired.

"It was good. *Real* good! I can understand why he was so bitter. If somebody had framed me and got me sent to prison, and *then* took my woman, I would feel the same way. But man, if he would've taken all the wisdom and wealth he obtained in prison and used it the right way... man."

"Sure," Boss agreed, pouring himself a cup of coffee and sitting at the desk. "But 'the Count' is real. It deals with real hurt and real emotions. In my opinion, love is the most powerful motivator in the world. People have written and sung about it for ages. Most of it is good and inspiring. But there are things that can happen to a man because of love that can render it an all-consuming evil," he said, shrugging his shoulders. "Edmond Dantes was in love. But Edmond Dantes died in prison. The man who swam out of that body bag was not in love; he was enraged! Revenge drove him. And he accomplished some great things. The tragedy is that his pursuit of revenge ended up costing him the very love that motivated the revenge in the first place."

"That's deep."

"Yeah, it is. It's a great book. One of my all-time favorites."

"What drives you, Boss?" Marcus asked inquisitively.

Boss chuckled. "That's a big question, lil bruh."

"Give me a big answer, then."

Boss thought about it for a second.

"It may be a little too 'spiritual' for somebody from your generation. You sure you wanna hear it?"

"As long as it's the truth, I do."

"Okay," he said, setting his cup down and grabbing an old, beat-up Bible off the shelf.

"This is what drives me," he said holding it up. "And not simply the book. I'm not one of those nutty fanatics who consider it a sin to sit a Bible on the floor. I'm driven by what this book reveals to me about the God who inspired the words in it to be written."

He could see a slight interest in Marcus' eyes, so he plodded on. "I was an awful person, man. You know, I was cool and people seemed to like me, but on the inside I was rotten. I didn't care about anyone but myself. The closest thing to love I experienced in the world was the relationship I shared with my wife. But at the time, it wasn't really love."

Marcus cut in, confused. "But you're still married?"

"Yeah, but we had to *learn* to love one another the right way. And we're still learning," he said, smiling. "Anyway, the day I got busted, I was shot up real bad. They didn't think I would make it. My wife, who was just my girlfriend at the time, got into the Bible real tough during this time. She told me she prayed and prayed, and promised God that if He let me survive, she would live for Him for the rest of her life. Essentially, she was giving up her life for mine," he said, pausing to reflect once again on this amazing blessing God had given him in Ebony.

"When I came out of the coma, she was a different person. It actually got on my nerves. I was facing a boat load of time. I needed my ride or die, but she kept talking about how God had spared my life. How Jesus had a purpose for me, and all that. I couldn't take it. I finally told her to roll."

"For real!" Marcus exclaimed, surprised.

"Yeah. Like I told you. I was rotten. And I wasn't trying to hear about Jesus' plans for me. I had my own plans, and they included me being out of prison. I needed lawyers. The kind that cost lots of money. So, I put my son's mother to work." He paused for a second when he saw how Marcus looked at him.

"I know, lil bruh. I was awful," he said, shrugging his shoulders, "Anyway, I lost at trial in the state. I thought the feds would leave me alone after that, but they didn't. I eventually copped out, figuring I would get the state time overturned on appeal. So, when I got to prison, I hit the ground running. I had a good run too, as far as those types of runs go. I made a lot of money in here. But every time they shot me down in appellate court, it took a little bit of fight out of me, and it took a lot of fight out of my son's mother. She ran off with close to thirty-five grand. I haven't heard from her since."

Boss threw his hands in the air and shrugged it off. Just part of the game.

"So, what happened? You still haven't answered my question," Marcus pushed.

"Ebony happened, lil bruh," he said with a grateful smile. "About three months after all of this went down she up and wrote me. Said she had been praying for me and thought I could use a friend. We kicked it for almost a year and she never brought up how things had ended between us. So, I finally asked her why. She answered the question by sending me a Bible, *this* Bible, and telling me to read 1 Corinthians 13. It got to me. She had something real, man. After that we started praying and studying together. In our letters, over the phone, in visit. I couldn't understand it at first, but the more I prayed and read, the more I understood. Once I realized what Christ had done for me, there was no turning back.

"I stopped looking at my sentence and started focusing on how I could spend the rest of my time on earth glorifying God. The closer I got to God, the more the Holy Spirit led me. Before I knew it, I was ministering throughout the prison. Because of how I used to get down, a lot of the staff here thought it was some kind of game I was running, but they eventually saw how sincere I was. God gave me favor with them, and they let me roam the compound freely whenever I needed. He's used me to minister to all the issues that life has to offer; addicts, bangers, homosexuals, racists, etc."

"So, God drives you?" Marcus commented, somewhat unsatisfied with the answer.

"Yes, but it's deeper than that," Boss said, closing his eyes and putting his hand on his temple as if in deep thought. "2 Corinthians 5:14-15 says, 'For the love of Christ controls us, because we have concluded this: that one has died for all, therefore all have died; and he died for all, that those who live might no longer live for themselves but for him who for their sake died and was raised.' See, I deserved to die, not just because I sold dope and hurt people. I deserved to die because I had lived my entire life in disobedience to God. I was a sinner, We're all sinners! The cost of sin is death. Christ died to pay off a debt I could never pay. That's love!

"Once the reality of that genuinely hit me, I couldn't go on living the way I was. I couldn't spit in the face of love like that. Not me! Not any longer! And it's that love that drives me."

Marcus sat there for a moment, staring at Boss and nodding his head in approval. "That's what's up, man. For real."

"So, what drives you?" Boss countered.

"I don't know. That's what I'm trying to figure out. Nothing really."

"Nothing?"

"Yeah, I mean, I just started thinking along those lines."

"Where are you going?" Boss inquired.

"What do you mean?" Marcus asked, confused.

"I mean, where do you see yourself five or ten years from now? What is your vision for your life?"

"I haven't thought that far ahead since the wreck," Marcus somberly replied.

"Well, in my experience, you'll never be driven if you don't know where you're going."

Marcus thought about it for a minute before responding. "You'll never be driven if you don't know where you're going." He repeated it to himself twice before finally saying, "Yeah, that's right," as if a light bulb was blinking over his head.

A few minutes later he left Boss' cell with Steve Jobs' biography by Walter Issacson and a lot to consider. *Where am I going?* he asked himself over and over again.

✝

The following week Marcus got a surprise visit from his mother. It was a surprise because she had not been to see him since the first visit. And even more of a surprise because she was alone.

When he walked into the visitation gallery, she was sitting in the row of chairs on the far wall staring out of one of the big windows. She was beautiful woman, but you could tell she was dealing with a lot on the inside. She didn't notice he had come in until he was standing over her.

"Mama."

"Hey, son," she said, standing up and giving him a warm hug.

"Did you find what you were looking for out there?" he joked.

"No, I didn't," she responded with a good-natured smile. "I found what I was looking for in here," she said, reaching for his hand

and squeezing it with the love only a mother can give. Marcus was encouraged, and nearly in tears as he looked into his mother's eyes. This is the mother he had always known. This is the mother he needed during this difficult time in his life.

"Son, I know I haven't made this easy for you!"

"I'm good, Mama," he interrupted.

"No, you're not, son. You're coping. I know because I was simply coping, But I woke up at three o'clock this morning and cried out to the Lord." She paused for a moment, choked up. "I've been crying and praying since the accident happened. And that gave me the strength to cope with it. But this morning, I cried out to God and asked Him to restore what was broken in my family. My prayer wasn't about me; it was about us. Your father and I lost a son. You and your sister lost a brother, and friend," she said, squeezing his hand again.

"We all lost," she continued, "and it hurts. Still, we have been blessed with so much, and we have so much to be thankful for." She closed her eyes and squeezed a little tighter.

"And what I realized this morning in prayer is that for all the crying I had done for the son I lost, I haven't been doing enough crying for you and for what you must be going through. I haven't been thankful enough for my son who survived."

Marcus threw his arm around his mother and drew her close. They stayed like that for the next forty-five minutes. Neither said a word. They just cried, and in their own way told God thank you.

CHAPTER 14

"**B**oyd! They're calling for you!" The officer screamed.

"Alright!" Silence yelled back, with a huge smile on his face. Boss, Marcus, JG, and a few others were gathered outside of his cell door. "Well..." he said, looking at the faces and emotions surrounding him. Then he looked directly at Boss and said, "Man, I wish I could take you with me."

"Yeah. But it ain't my season. It's yours," Boss said with a smile. "Let me get a quick word with you before you roll, E."

Boss stepped into the cell while Silence shared a few more handshakes and hugs. When he was finished, he walked into the cell, pulling the door up behind him. "What's up, Boss?"

"I don't believe it's necessary, but I'ma say this anyway."

"I already know, big bruh," Silence said, cutting him off, "Live!"

"Live!" Boss repeated, passionately. "And don't let that young girl who's been lying to you, telling you that you still 'got it' trip you up," he added, smiling.

"I ain't gon let her trip me up, but I got other plans for her, preacher," Silence responded, laughing.

"Alright, man," Boss said laughing, "get up out of here."

"Love you, big bruh," Silence said, hugging the man who had been the closest person in his life for nearly a decade.

"Love you, too, man."

†

It had been six months since Silence went home, and Marcus was still finding it difficult to adjust to his absence. JG had moved into the cell with him, but he was not equipped to be the big brother Silence had been. He was a respectful celly, but when it came to personal issues, he was not the person you wanted to share them with. He had too many issues of his own he was still struggling to deal with. So, Marcus kept a lot bottled up.

He was lying on the bottom bunk with his headphones on listening to the radio when JG walked in.

"What's up, celly? They called big yard. You rolling with me?"

"Why? What you about to do? Workout?" Marcus asked, surprised.

"Nah, I'ma shoot some ball," JG said, putting on his new Nikes.

"You can't even hoop, dude!"

"Bruh, you really gotta stop hating on me. It doesn't look good on you."

"It isn't hating if it's true."

"Look, I know I ain't Lebron or KD. But I'm better than most of them dudes who gon be on the court out there," he said, defending his game. "But it really doesn't matter, as long as I look good doing it. That Chamberlain broad gon be out there."

"But you can't hoop! Them dudes gon shine on you out there," Marcus said, getting off the bunk. "You know what? I'm going. I need a good laugh."

"You still don't get it, do you?" JG said, with a suave smile on his face. "Bruh, I'm a PTPer."

"A what?"

"Prime Time Performer! When the bright lights come on, and the crowd is ready for a show, I turn up!"

"Prime Time Performer," Marcus said, sarcastically.

"Homie, with gal out there watching, I'll mess around and bang one."

"Bang one! You can't even smack boards."

"Prime Time Performer," JG said, walking out of the door. Marcus followed, looking forward to the show.

✝

When they returned from the big yard, Lil D was leaning on the rail in front of their door waiting for them. The saddened look on his face told them both that something bad had happened.

"What's up, D? What's wrong, man?" JG asked, a little worried.

He just shook his head. "Go holler at Boss, bruh."

"What wrong?" Marcus inquired.

"He'll tell you."

They hurried to Boss' cell. When they got there, he was sitting back on the bunk, crying. Whatever it was, it had to be real bad. They had never seen Boss show this kind of emotion.

"What's going on, big bruh?" JG asked anxiously.

"They killed him, man," he responded, heartbroken.

"Who? Killed who!?" Marcus cried, but he knew.

Boss looked up at the two young brothers for the first time since they had entered the room. His eyes said it all. He was crushed. "E, man," he said between whimpers. "They gunned him down out there, man."

"Nah, man. Nah!" Marcus pleaded, tears already streaming down his face as he stormed out of the cell, angrily slamming the door. JG started to go after him, but Boss stopped him.

"Let him go, lil bruh. He's hurt. He needs to be left alone for a minute." JG was still shocked. He knew how vicious that gang life was, but he had always considered Silence to be untouchable. The price was too steep to cross someone of his status. Or at least that's what he had assumed.

"What happened, man? How did it happen?"

"I don't know how, but I was hearing rumors about it an hour ago, so I got on the phone. His girl told my wife it was his own homeboys who did it." You could hear the contempt in his voice.

"What?! Nah, not him. Them dudes love Silence."

"Everything we call love ain't love, lil bruh. True enough, he had a lot of influence out there, but he had been gone a long time. In prison you live in close quarters with your so-called enemies. You get to see their humanity. You earn a level of respect for them as a person." He paused, considering his own prior affiliation, and he and Silence had clicked. "Sometimes you even build relationships with them," he continued. "But it's different out there. Your enemy is simply a title, a tag, a color, or a neighborhood. A target. Their humanity is non-existent. A big game hunter doesn't respect the bear he kills. He shoots it, chops off its head, and hangs it on the wall as a trophy." He shook his head, amazed at the savagery of man.

"So," he continued, "when he got out, talking about making peace treaties, building alliances to uplift the community, and stuff like that, he was speaking a foreign language. A language this younger generation neither understands nor respects. To them it's perceived as weak and unprofitable. And because he had been gone so long, when push came to shove, they just got rid of him."

"Politics," JG whispered, almost as an afterthought.

Boss was surprised. "Yep," he responded, "that's exactly what it was. And as usual, the government wins, and the people lose."

Marcus didn't talk much for a couple of weeks after Silence's murder. He spent most of his time in the cell reading or in the library studying. Even when he went to the yard, he got off to himself, in his own thoughts. He and Silence had grown very close. He felt like he had lost a brother. Again.

JG was also saddened but being in the streets had made him less sensitive to death in a sense. In the game it was normal, typical, and even expected. Kill or be killed. Ride or die. Cradle to the grave. So, he moved on, more aware of his own mortality, but unshaken.

Lil D and Silence had never formed too tight of a bond. That isn't to say they weren't cool. They had lived in the same pod together for a few years and associated with a lot of the same people. So, their paths crossed often, where the communication was always cordial and respectful. Lil D really admired Silence's drive and intelligence. He couldn't understand how someone so bright could end up so bound to a lifestyle that would never allow him to fulfill his potential. For him, Silence's death was more motivation to take advantage of the gifts and talents he had been blessed with.

Boss took it the worst, of course. He had lost a family member. A close one. No doubt about it Boss, in some capacity, filled the role of advisor and/or mentor to most of the men he associated with in prison., including Silence. But very few had garnered enough of his respect to counsel him from time to time. Silence was one of the few. Or E, as he called him. He'd never liked the moniker. Why would a voice as powerful as his ever remain silent? Therefore, he had always encouraged him to use his influence to affect change. Which, as is often the case, led to his death.

He had even introduced him to Ebony in visit, something that occurred as frequently as Jubilee. And because of that, she had likewise embraced him as family. Thus, for him, this was a family tragedy. However, because of his unwavering faith, he was able to deal with it maturely. Something Marcus really needed and appreciated.

He had been dropping by the cell to check on Marcus every day. Today was no exception. He was leaning on the top-tier rail in front of his door looking out over the unit when Boss walked up.

"What's happening, lil bruh?"

"What's up, Boss?" he replied, thoughts still somewhere else.

"Not too much, man," he said, leaning on the rail next to him. "How's your family doing?"

"They're good, big bruh," Marcus answered. "Looking forward to me coming home next year. I am too."

"You better be," Boss encouraged." Are you still working on your master plan?"

"Oh, yeah. That's mandatory. But I've also been putting together something new. A non-profit."

"Yeah," Boss replied, impressed by how knowledgeable this young man was. "What kind is it?"

"It's geared toward reaching 'troubled' youth through academics, arts, and trades before they are gobbled up by things like drugs and gangs. Or sheer hopelessness."

"That's commendable, lil bruh," he said, looking at Marcus with a newfound respect. "Ambitious; but very commendable. And needed."

"Yeah, I think so. I'm calling it 'Redeeming Silence,'" he reflectively commented. "It's crazy, Boss. I was in the cell with him for three years, and if I hadn't known he was the leader of a gang, the thought never would've crossed my mind. All he did was show me love. Treated me like a little brother the entire time. Not once did he impose his 'rep' on me. Ever! And the dude was so intelligent. He would've been successful at whatever he chose to do. Would've been," he almost whispered.

"Man, don't I know it," Boss agreed.

"That's why I wanna do this. I *need* to do this. Because there are a lot more people just like him out there in the streets, or in juvenile facilities, who need mentors like you and him to make personal investments in their lives. They need someone to show them that there is hope in this world. They need to know what lies within. Before it's too late."

"Preach, young brother! And remember, they don't just need the testimony and guidance of old hardened dudes like me. Your voice is just as relevant. If not more relevant."

"I don't know, man," Marcus responded doubtfully.

"You don't know? Come on, man. You're smart. Or do you suppose that 'troubled youth' only live in neighborhoods, or grew up in families where drugs and gangs are prevalent? You got dudes walking around you every day in here who grew up in nice neighborhoods with respectful families. Some were raised by college graduates, pastors, police officers, teachers, doctors, etc. They weren't troubled in the same ways children who were raised in drug and gang infested environments were, yet they were troubled all the same. Trouble comes in all types of forms. It can come in the form of your daddy being in prison and your mother being on crack. Or it can come in the form of a sick family member violating your innocence. It can come looking like Satan or looking like a savior, but it's all trouble. We all have different stories. Therefore, if you want this to reach 'troubled youth' you need to be able to identify and relate to all kinds of trouble."

"Yeah," Marcus was slowly nodding his head, "you're right. So," he said, smiling, "when we gon start working on this?"

Boss just looked at him and let out a hearty chuckle. He knew he was locked in. "We already have, lil bruh. We already have."

CHAPTER 15

"What's up, Lil D?" JG almost screamed into the phone.

"J! What's up, man?"

"How're things going out there, man?"

"Fast! Man, running a business is hard work, dude. Especially stepping into it fresh out of prison."

"You ain't complaining, are you?"

"Nah, man. It's hard, but I know how blessed I am. Pops had everything set for me. All I had to do was hire employees. We opened up shop last week."

"That's what's up, fool," JG said, happy for his friend's success. "How is your fam?"

"They're cool, man. Mama got a lil more life in her now. She still missing Pops but having me out here has given her a boost. Sis crazy, man! She don't wanna let me out of her sight. Been trying to fix me up with one of her friends at church to keep tabs on me." They both laughed.

"How have you been doing, man?" Lil D inquired.

"I'm good, fool."

"When you meet the board?"

"Man, I'm good on that. I wrote and told em to take me off the docket. Forever!"

"What?" Lil D was dumbfounded. "Why?"

"Man, I flatten out in eight months."

"So what?"

"So, what! Man, I ain't bout to let them folks keep they hooks in me."

"You plan on violating?"

"Nah. I don't plan on coming back at all. But I don't know what might happen, so..."

"You tripping, J."

"Maybe. You know you can't put nothing past me. But I feel like this is the right move for me."

"Okay," Lil D relented. "How your family *feel* about it?"

"Mixed reviews. My Aunt Trish gon support me no matter what. She just wanna see me do good for myself. Tina a nutcase. She always gon have something crazy to say. Jessica don't like it, but she finally starting to believe in me. So, when I told her I made this decision with *our* best interest in mind, she rode with it."

"Did you?" Lil D asked, skeptically.

"Did I what?"

"Make the decision with their best interest in mind?"

"Absolutely!" he answered with conviction. "No joking bruh, I'm in the cell with a real monster. Silence's death brought out something in Marcus he didn't know was there. Lil dude gon be a millionaire philanthropist one day. Me, him, and Boss be in the cell or on the big yard chopping it up, and all kinds of ideas come out of it. I'm thinking on levels I didn't know existed for me, fool. I used to read *Entrepreneur* magazines and think that stuff was for other people. Now I feel like it's just a matter of time before I'm on the *cover*," he finished passionately.

"Okay," Lil D said nodding his head. "My bad. I see you, JG Rockafella!"

"Now you feeling me, homie! Man, I been ready to leave since the day I got here. I would have been straight if I'd have never met your dime bag buying, garbage weed smoking, ash tray roach stealing—"

"Hey, man! I got feelings too, bruh," Lil D interrupted, smiling on the other end of the phone.

"You know I'm just messing with you, fool," JG said, smiling as well. "But being here right now is preparing me to be an example to my son that he can be proud of when I do get out of here. To me, that makes a few more months here worth it."

✝

That Saturday Boss, JG, and Marcus all went to visit. They hadn't planned it, but it gave them the opportunity to introduce their families to one another. Though they dispersed afterward to enjoy the little time they had with their loved ones, at the end of visit they met back up and let Boss lead them all in a prayer before they left.

The next day they decided to pitch in and put a meal together. JG had become a pretty decent cook as far as prison goes, and whipped up some tuna croquettes, cream corn, mac and cheese, and green beans. For dessert, he made a banging peppermint cheesecake. They found an empty table out on the pod where they ate and kicked it for the next couple of hours.

"Compliments to the chef, J. You took me back to those Sunday dinners we used to have when I was a youngster."

"Appreciate that, Bossman. I can't wait to get in the kitchen and shock the fam with one of my creations when I get out. Gordon Ramsey style."

"Aw, man. Here we go," Marcus said, shaking his head.

"What you mean, 'here we go'?" JG responded, in full character. "I'm learning essential lessons from Chef Ramsey and the crew as I continue to progress toward culinary excellence."

"'Culinary excellence.' Cut it out, man."

"Don't hate, Lil Marcus. I enjoy learning how to cook, something my woman will appreciate. You enjoy learning how to kill zombies. If there was ever an attack, I'm sure your woman would be grateful."

"That's cold," Boss chimed in laughing.

"Bruh," Marcus replied imperviously, "I'm well past the point of you being able to make fun of me for watching *The Walking Dead.* I'm junked all the way out!"

"Ya'll silly, man," Boss said, leaning forward on the stool and putting his elbows on the table. It was time to talk some business. "So where are we at on this project?"

"Well, I got the rest of those letters in the mail this morning. Now we're just waiting to see who responds," Marcus replied, hopeful.

"Okay. How about on your end, J?"

"Jessica spoke to someone from Another Way on Friday. She told me they didn't get to talk very long, but whoever it was said he would call her back when he had the time to answer her questions. I'll let y'all know when I hear something," he said, then added, "oh, and Lil D told me that whatever we need him to do to help, he got us."

"That's alright, man," Boss voiced, grateful for the help. "It's good to hear he's doing good out there. So, Ebony has been talking to that lawyer about filing all the paperwork. She already paid him, so we don't have to worry about that."

"What! Nah, Bossman. We can't let you do that," JG exclaimed.

"He's right, big bruh. That's not fair to you and Ebony. We're in this together. Equally!" Marcus added.

Boss was touched. "I know, lil brothers. But we've been blessed. We finally got my appeal lawyer paid off, so when my baby got her income tax check, she wanted to do this. When she makes up her mind to do something..." he cut it short, shrugging his shoulders.

"That's what's up, big bruh. Make sure you let her know we appreciate it," JG expressed.

"Yeah, man," Marcus agreed.

"She knows," Boss assured them.

"So," JG ventured, uneasily, "what's going on with your appeal?"

"Man, you know how that goes. They give us thirty-day deadlines to file and give them an indefinite amount of time to answer."

"What's your lawyer saying?" Marcus interjected.

"The only thing he can say. But I'm used to it."

"What are you looking for them to do?"

"Well, it's gotten to the point now where I could care less if they overturn my state case or not. I'm almost done with it. What I really need em to do is rule that my fed time should have been running with my state time."

"How likely is it that they'll do it?" JG asked.

"It's not unprecedented; but it's not something they usually do either," Boss answered realistically. "But right now, it's the only shot I got. So I'ma shoot it."

At that, the conversation ceased. Talking about sentences as lengthy as Boss' usually brought on a somber mood. Even more so when it was someone who so obviously deserved a second chance.

"Alright y'all," Boss said with a warm smile, "the funeral is over. Let's stay focused on taking our communities back so that fewer of us have to ever worry about filing an appeal."

"Alright, then. What's next?" JG asked.

"Hey man, y'all know I'm in this thing one hundred percent," Marcus quipped, looking at his watch, "but it's Sunday night. *The Walking Dead* about to come on, so..."

They all got a kick out of this and could only conclude that it was time to call it a day. Marcus went to the cell to tune in, JG hopped on the phone, and Boss, ever the servant, grabbed all the dirty dishes.

"Ebony? Can you hear me? Hello?"

"Hello! Otis."

"Yeah, I'm here. Can you hear me?" Boss asked, a little annoyed.

"Yeah, I hear you now, baby. Whew, this phone gets on my *nerves*!" Ebony exclaimed.

"You've been saying that for two months now."

"I *know*! I've been so busy." She sounded spent.

"If you're so busy that you don't have time to take care of something that's getting on your nerves, you're too busy, baby," Boss said, voice stern.

"I know, Otis. I know," she yielded, knowing where this was going if she didn't take action. "And I give you my word that when you call me tomorrow, I'll have a new phone. Okay, *Mr.* Hamilton?" she said, sarcastically.

"Keep on!" he shot back, smiling. It still amazed him how great of a relationship they had maintained throughout all these years. They had faced so much together. Been pushed to the limits on numerous occasions. But their commitment to God and one another always prevailed.

"Keep on, what?" She was poking at him now. "What you gon do, Mr. Hamilton?" she continued, laughing.

"Woman, you lucky I love you."

"No, I'm not! I'm blessed! And so are you!"

"Yes, I am, *Mrs.* Hamilton. So how was work today?"

"Ugh," she expressed, as if the thought itself annoyed her. "I called myself doing Veronica a favor by letting Tae run some errands, clean up around the shop, stuff like that. But the girl act like she crazy or something. Baby, I send her to pick up some hair products from Ms. Jin, and it took her an hour to get back. I asked her what took so long, and guess what this girl tells me?"

"What?" Otis asked facetiously.

Ebony laughed. "I'm being serious, Otis. Guess what this girl told me?"

"What, baby?" he repeated, trying not to laugh.

"This girl told me she didn't know I needed her to come right back, so she stopped by her boyfriend's place!"

"Oh yeah?"

"Yeah, but that ain't all. The girl was high, baby! She went over there to smoke a joint, or whatever it is they smoke now. I couldn't believe it!"

"At least she came back," he joked.

"Otis!"

"Hold on, baby. I'm not making excuses for the girl. If you didn't already fire her, you have every right to. But you had to know what you were getting into when you hired her. Look at her mama! I know that's your sister but, hey, there's one in every family."

"Yeah," she agreed.

"But you did it anyway. And I suspect you did it because you don't want her to turn out like Veronica. So be patient. You gotta put your foot down, of course. Especially that getting high on the job stuff. That's totally unacceptable. But don't give up on her. The less time she spends around her mama, and the more time she is around you, the better chance she has of making something out of her life."

"Yeah, you're right," she consented. "But that girl—"

"Baby," Boss interrupted, "there can't be any buts."

She took a deep breath. He was right, as usual. They sometimes gave one another a hard time, but in the end one or the other would graciously submit to the truth. In their relationship, truth always reigned. *That's what is keeping us going*, Ebony thought. You can "love" someone upon false pretenses and see it all come tumbling down. However, when the love you share is founded upon the truth, no storm you face can topple what you have.

"I know, baby. Thank you," she calmly stated. As she rounded the corner, she noticed a car parked in her driveway and a young man sitting on the front porch texting on his phone.

"There's somebody here," she said, eyeing him suspiciously as she slowly pulled into the driveway.

"Who?" Boss asked, alert.

"I don't know, but it looks like..." she stopped short, shocked.

"Ebony! Who is it?!"

"Baby, it's Prince," she whispered, getting out of the car.

"What?!" Boss was stunned into silence. Ebony approached the man sitting on the porch and gave him a warm but awkward hug as he stood up.

"Hey, Prince. It's good to see you."

"Yeah, it's good to see you too, Ebony."

"So, what's going on? You want to come in?"

"Nah, not tonight. I just come over to ask you to tell my daddy I need to see him."

"He's, uh, on the phone right now if you want to talk to him," she said reaching the phone out to him.

"Nah, I need to see him face to face. Do they still get special visits?"

"Yes, they do. I'll let him know."

"Alright. Thank you, Ebony," he said, walking to his car.

"Oh, Prince!" She hollered. "When do you want him to put in for the visit? What day?"

"Im in town for the next two weeks, so..."

She said something into the phone and hollered back, "Next Saturday, okay?"

"Yeah. Just Facebook me to let me know what time."

"Okay. Good night, Prince."

"Good night," he replied as he got into his car.

"Otis?"

"Yeah, I'm here, baby."

"You ok?"

"Yeah, I'm good." But you could tell he was still in shock.

"I wonder what he wants to talk about that he didn't want to talk about on the phone?"

"I don't know. But whatever it is, it's long overdue," he said, already praying for God to give him the words to say.

Boss had not seen his son in nearly twenty years. It's been close to twelve years since they'd had any communication. After Prince's mother, Crystal, ran off with Boss' money, she eventually left town. Boss had no idea where they'd gone. A couple of years later Ebony had run into them at the mall. They were in town for the holidays visiting Crystal's family. If it had been up to Crystal, they would've walked right past one another without a second glance. She still couldn't stand Ebony. But Prince adored her. Always had. And when you're a child, the petty grudges adults engage in are not impressive enough for you to get involved in. So, he ran over to give Ebony a big hug.

He asked her if she had talked to his dad and why he hadn't called him. She could see how confusing it all was for him, feeling like he knew his father loved him but not understanding why he never called. Ebony could only imagine what lies Crystal had fed him about Otis, and it broke her heart that she couldn't tell him the truth. So, she simply assured him that his father loved him dearly and was always thinking about him. He asked his mother if it was okay to give Ebony her phone number just in case his father had lost it, something Ebony found interesting. She knew for a fact Otis had never had the number, but she wouldn't say that to him. However, she did give Crystal a knowing glance that was difficult to keep from becoming a glare.

Crystal was unaffected. She played it cool and gave Ebony her cell phone number. Then she told Prince they had to get going and off they went. It took Boss a few days to call after that encounter because the prison had been on lock down. As soon as he found out, he told Ebony to call on three-way. No answer. He left a message that never received a response. They called several times over the next few months, but no one ever answered. The last time they called, the number was out of service. Boss was heartbroken, but there was nothing he could do.

Now his son, who had been forced to grow into manhood without his father, stood before him.

Putting his personal opinion of Crystal to the side, Boss could see that she had done a pretty good job of raising him. He was well-groomed and appeared to be well-mannered. Despite the raw emotions he had to be experiencing, he seemed to be very composed. *That's my contribution,* he thought. Neither man knew what the appropriate greeting was for a father and son under these circumstances, so they settled on a manly handshake before sitting down right across from one another.

"So," Boss said, breaking the ice, "how are you, son?" It came out natural, but it made the encounter more intense for both of them. *Man,* Boss thought, *it shouldn't be this hard! This is my son!*

"I'm good," Prince responded, staring across the table at the man he had both loved and hated more passionately than anyone else he'd ever known. At that moment he didn't really know what he felt.

"You look good. I can see you've been taking care of yourself."

"Yeah, I try."

Boss let out a deep sigh, shrugging his shoulders and shaking his head. "Prince, you gon have to help me out here. I know this is difficult for you, but it's also difficult for me. It's been twelve years, man. What do you want me to say?"

Prince thought about it for a second. He had rehearsed this scene a couple of times, but things weren't going as he planned. "I don't know, man. I just wanna know what happened?"

Boss shook his head again and looked him dead in his eyes. "Look, so..." He couldn't bring himself to say it.

"Pops," Prince replied, surprised by how good it felt to address this man by that title. "You don't have to protect my mama. She told me it wasn't all your fault. She wouldn't tell me anything else, but she is the one who suggested I get in contact with you."

"Really?" Boss was shocked... and grateful.

"Yeah. She's softening up in her old age," he said with a smile. *He has his mother's smile*, Boss thought. *And he really loves her.*

"So, what is it you want to know?" Boss asked, already calculating what to share and what he would withhold. There was no need to inflict any more wounds or cause any further separation. It was time for healing and reconciliation.

"I wanna know what happened, man!" he said, showing the first signs of emotions.

Boss could relate. His father had not been in his life either, always running the streets. He would occasionally pick Boss up on a Saturday afternoon, take him to see his Granny, and drop him back off five dollars richer. But that was it. When Boss was a teenager and venturing into the streets himself, they crossed paths more often. However, by this time Boss viewed him less as a father and more as a dude on the block a lot of people looked up to. Or feared.

When he was fifteen his father had tried to discipline him for skipping school to hang out in the projects. Boss and a group of friends were standing around smoking a joint when his dad walked up.

"Otis, let's go," his father said. Boss ignored him. His friends knew his dad didn't play, so they began to slowly scatter.

"Boy, you heard me! Let's go!"

"I ain't your boy! And I ain't going nowhere with you!" Boss spat out, attempting to growl.

"Oh yeah," his dad said, finding his revolt humorous. "So, you a man now, huh? You a man! I said let's go, lil nig..."

He reached out to grab Boss by the arm, but at the same time Boss was reaching for the pistol he now kept on him at all times. His father stepped back, shocked.

"Oh! Now you a killa?" His father was laughing. "You a killa, huh? You gon shoot me? You gon gun your pops down out here?"

"You ain't my daddy, man! You ain't never been a daddy to me! I hate you!" Boss screamed.

"Okay," his dad said, nodding his head, facial expression changing. "Okay. So ... if I'm not your father ... and you're not my son ... I need to be taking this seriously, huh," his face and voice were now menacing.

Boss was a little scared now. He really hated him. At least he felt like he did. But he didn't really want to shoot him. He had never shot anybody. He had never shot *at* anyone. He was just mad. But now he found himself standing out here, gun drawn on his own father, a man who was known to be about the business. Just then his sister ran up, screaming.

"Otis, put that down! Daddy, what y'all doing! Stop!" She cried out.

Her voice brought both of them back from their lunacy. She stepped in between them, and Boss lowered the gun. He and his father stared at each other for what seemed like thirty minutes, but it was only about ten seconds. His dad nodded his head at him, kissed his daughter, and walked away. That was the last time he saw his father alive. He was killed in a car crash fleeing from the police three days later. He always regretted never being able to make amends. He wouldn't miss another opportunity to do so.

CHAPTER 16

The next six months went by in a blur. Boss was focused on reclaiming some semblance of a healthy relationship with Prince. It was still a grind for each of them, but they had kept it. He and Crystal had even shared a cordial moment via speaker phone. JG spent the majority of his time reworking the financials in his business plan. He was really starting to see a future for himself in the world of entrepreneurship. Marcus found himself in the position that everyone in prison desires, but few are prepared for. He was about to walk back through the very gates that had once appeared to him to be a sentence of death. But he had made it. And he had not just *survived* prison. Because of the brothers and the mentors that he had been blessed with, he had become a man in a place that often times seemed to be intent on stripping you of your manhood.

They were now having round table discussions two or three days a week, for hours at a time. So much progress had been made on "Redeeming the Silence," as they now called it, that Ebony had found a group of community leaders from some of the local churches and organizations who were strongly considering supporting the movement. They were just waiting to meet with Marcus after he was released to make sure he would still be as invested in the vision as he was now. They obviously didn't know who they were dealing with.

"So, how are you feeling, lil bruh?" Boss asked Marcus.

"I'm good, big bruh. I mean, I'm a little nervous, but I think that's mostly due to the unknown of moving to a new city."

"Yeah, Boss, you gotta keep in mind that this dude was still living in his parents' house, with posters of LeBron and the Minions on his wall when he got locked up," JG clowned. "And he was probably a virgin, too," he added.

"Man, I wasn't no virgin!" Marcus replied laughing.

"But you did have a minions poster on your wall?"

"Nah! I had a poster of Tina on my wall!"

"Keep on! I told her you stole one of my pictures of her. She knows you on your way home. She gon put a restraining order on you."

"Man, you really told her that!" Marcus exclaimed, punching him in the arm.

"Yeah. I told you I was. But you straight fool. I think she likes it. I told you she crazy. You might have to put a restraining order on her."

"You stupid, man," Boss said, smiling. "Anyway, you got everything in order?"

"Yeah," Marcus assured him. "My folks are already up here. They're staying in a hotel tonight, so they'll be here bright and early in the morning."

"That's what's up," JG remarked.

"Yeah. I had wanted to ride the bus, but I'm glad they changed my mind."

"Yeah, because you were tripping," JG said frowning up.

"Anyway," Marcus went on, knowing he would miss these men the moment he left them. They were family. And though they would undoubtedly be in regular contact, and may very well meet up on the outside, he questioned if it would ever be like this again. This could be a very special community if you valued and nurtured it.

"Well," Boss said, standing up to leave their cell, "I need to get down here tand call the wife before lockdown. I'll see you lil brothers in the morning, Lord willing. Love you, man," he announced, hugging each of them.

"Alright, big bruh. Love you, too, man." Marcus replied, almost tearing up.

"Love, Boss man," JG said, wondering why he was emotional as well.

✝

Later that night Marcus lay on the top bunk staring at the ceiling. JG was on the bottom bunk uninterestedly watching an episode of *Bar Rescue*. It amazed him that people waited until they were half a million dollars in the red before they called for help. *Crazy*, he thought. A commercial came on and he started flipping through channels. When he did, Marcus hopped off the top bunk and walked to the door to look out of the window.

"What's up, lil bruh?" JG said, smiling. "If you're planning on posting up right there until the morning you got a long way to go."

"Man!" He grabbed his watch off the shelf. It was just 10:30 pm. "I always hear people talking about how hard it was to get to sleep the night before they went home, and I thought it was foolishness. Silence was sleep by 9:30 and didn't wake up until 5:00 the next morning. Just like any other day."

"Yeah, but he was not just any other dude. He was a different breed."

"Huh. That's an understatement."

"When was the last time you talked to his brother," JG inquired.

"A couple days ago," Marcus replied. "I'm supposed to get with him next weekend some time. Since I'll be living down there, he wants to help me put this thing together. To honor the life his brother could've had."

"That's what's up."

"Yeah, I'm looking forward to it, man. I hope having him with us makes the transition easier," he stated, carefully measuring his words.

"I really do thank God for Ebony. She's a blessing. But he's closer to my age. We've got more in common; you know?"

"I feel you." JG sat up and rolled out of the bunk, picking up a glass of water he had sitting on the desk. "So, your folks are actually cool with this?" he questioned, doubtfully.

"They are, but they aren't. I've been away from them for almost five years. They've been anticipating this day for a long time. So, me telling them that instead of coming back home, I'm moving four hours away, it hurts a little bit and I hate it. But I have to do this, man!"

"Yeah. Once they see how much good it does, they'll understand."

"Oh, they get that already. I was talking to my mama the other day. She said she did some research on how much time people with charges similar to mine usually spent in prison. It blew her mind. Blacks were five times more likely to be sentenced to prison time than whites, who usually received probation. That led to more research." He paused to look at his watch again: 10:45. Time was standing still, he thought. JG laughed.

"Anyway. Now, I had no criminal record to speak of. I was on my way to college, literally. The 'victim' was my brother, who was a passenger in my car. Before that night, there was no history of drug use. Do you know how many whites in this state with similar, and even worse situations, have served a day in prison?"

"Probably none," JG answered, matter-of-factly.

"Exactly! None! That helped her to see how important it is for us to reach our youth before it's too late. Before one mistake ruins the rest of their lives."

"Yeah, I agree. But when you look at it, it didn't ruin your life," JG observed.

"Okay. Yours either. But it's thousands of us in juvenile facilities, jails, and prisons. What percentage of those come out of this better?"

"Not many," JG sadly acknowledged.

"Right. Not many. But if they never have to go through this. If they never hit the blunt, or pick up the pack, or join the affiliation…"

"Or shoot dice or crash the car," JG finished.

"Come on, man! That's our mission. To keep them from making the mistakes we made. To channel that energy toward things more productive."

JG looked at Marcus with genuine admiration. There were only a few people in the world he truly respected. None more so than this soon to be twenty-three-year-old who had somehow discovered life in the midst of death.

"So, how long are you staying up there with them before you make your move?"

"Until Sunday. My dad is going to drive me down there on Monday, spend the night and drive back. After that, it's all business."

"Alright. It sounds like you got everything in order."

"Well," Marcus said, nodding his head, "we'll see."

"Good. Now hop back up on that bunk and go to sleep. Some of us gotta go to work in the morning," JG said laying back down and turning off the television.

Marcus was released the next morning with nowhere near the fanfare Silence had received. Boss and JG were there to see him off. But his stay in prison had gone unnoticed by the majority of his "peers." To many of them he was known either as "Silence's celly" or "JG's celly" or "lil young dude who be studying with Boss." To them, he had no name or identity of his own. He was a nobody. Yet, whether they knew it or not, their imprint on him had been massive. And the mark he would make in many of their communities would be even bigger.

CHAPTER 17

Since Marcus had left, a minor tension had formed between Boss and JG. Boss had been in prison for a long time and was accustomed to having close friends leave him. It came with the territory. There was a bittersweet sting to it, but the only thing to do was move on.

JG's situation was different. When he was in the game, it appeared that he had lots of friends. There were always hustlers, moochers, slicksters, and the occasional monster devotedly hanging around trying to get a piece of the action. But, as to be expected, when there was no more action, there were no more "friends" hanging around. Lil D, Boss, Silence and Marcus had become his everyday circle. Now Boss was all he had, and he expected him to make up for the loss of the rest of them. Yet, as much as Boss sympathized with him, he could not give JG all his time and attention. He was on the big yard setting up the squat rack when JG walked up.

"What's up, Bossman?" he said with a smile.

"What's going on, J?" Boss was surprised to see JG on the weight pile. "You must be lost, man. The basketball court is over there," he said sarcastically. They both laughed.

"Man, who you telling! I ain't touched a weight in bout three years. But I got a few months left and I gotta at least *look* like I been in here getting money."

"So, you're going to kill yourself for a few months in order to make people think you've been working out the whole time?"

"Yeah! I'm sticking to the script," he jokingly said.

"Alright, then," Boss replied, not comprehending that mentality. He started loading weight on the bar. JG began to help him, looking around.

"Where your workout partner at, big bruh?"

"I don't know, man," he commented, eyeballing the gate you had to come through in order to get to the big yard. "After yesterday, he might be having second thoughts."

JG laughed. "Man, how many dudes have you ran off since Silence?"

"Ah man, it's too many to count. They think they're ready, but they ain't built like E. He almost made me tap one day, but I would've blacked out first." He laughed, remembering the fondness of the fellowship they had enjoyed working out.

"You wanna jump in?" he asked, giving JG a challenging look.

"Maaannn," JG said with a tinge of fear, "on *leg* day? You trying to bust me up, big bruh."

"I'm trying to build you up. You gotta start somewhere. But it's your call," he concluded, stepping into the squat rack to warm up.

"Alright. But I can't lift what you're lifting."

"I don't expect you to. All I expect, or better yet, all I *require* if you gon work out with me is that you give everything you got."

"That might not be much."

"Lil bruh, I've been around you for a while now. Trust me, you've got more in you than you know."

Afterwards, as was Boss' habit, they walked some laps around the track. To JG, every step was excruciating. "Man, I don't know what I was thinking. I ain't gon be able to sit on the toilet for three days."

"Sitting down won't be too bad. Now, getting back up ... that's gon be a problem," Boss said, smiling.

"Oh, that's funny to you?"

"A lil bit. And only because I've been there, lil bruh."

"You? Yeah right!" JG exclaimed, skeptical.

"What? You think I came out of the womb doing thrusters?"

"Yeah!" JG shouted. "And walking lunges!"

"You silly, lil bruh," Boss replied, laughing. "Man, I don't care who you are. Nobody starts at the top of nothing!"

"What about them kids with rich parents. They grow up with everything they could ever want. And then, when they become adults, they either shoot straight to the top of daddy's business or start their own."

"You really think that's starting out on top?"

"Yeah! You don't?" JG asked incredulously.

"No, I don't," Boss responded. "How many of them actually last? Most of em end up running the company into the ground. Or before they do, daddy steps in and takes the reins back."

"So what? They're still rich."

"Nah. Daddy or mommy or both are rich. And because they are, their children benefit from it. But not understanding what it took for their parents to obtain the wealth, although they benefit from it they never fully appreciate it.

When I first started working out, I was just like you. Man, dudes saw how big I was and expected me to be able to pick up everything on the weight pile. I knew I was physically strong, so when they asked me what I wanted on the bench press, I told em just to throw something on there. Two seventy-five almost killed me," Boss remembered, chuckling. "It was a hit to my pride, and I almost gave it up. I was strong enough to prove my point if anybody got wrong. But a few more experienced dudes pulled me over. Once they showed me *how* to work out right, it was a rap. I committed myself to getting it five days a week: rain, sleet, or snow. And because of that I can appreciate what it takes to get there."

"You think I can do that in three months?" JG joked.

"Nah, man," Boss answered, smiling "But three months of dedication could build something *in you* that will positively impact every area of your life."

"So, you can't turn me into a beast in three months? Cause I already told Tina, 'I'ma be a beast by the time I touch down.'"

"You might wanna tell her to lower her expectations a lil bit, lil bruh."

"To what? A monster?"

"Not quite, lil bruh. Maybe a baby monster."

"Nah. That don't even sound right, Boss. How bout an *animal*?"

"What *kind* of animal?" Boss inquired, having fun with it.

"Not a kind of animal, Boss. Just an animal!"

"That's a stretch, bruh. But we'll see," Boss said, shifting gears. "Anyway, how have you been doing, lil bruh?" He was genuinely concerned.

"I'm straight," he responded, putting up his defense.

"Come on lil bruh. You've been a lil throwed off since your celly went home," Boss remarked with a chuckle.

"Yeahhh, man, I'm good. I know I been getting on your nerves, big bruh."

"It's cool, man. I get it. Good company is a valuable asset, and I know this isn't the easiest place to find it. There are a lot of bitter, negative dudes in here. You're doing right by staying away, especially being as close as you are to walking out of here. Some of these dudes in here hate to see somebody else doing good."

"Man, that's exactly how I was feeling. You bout the only one left who I know gon keep me walking straight."

"Nah, don't give me more credit than I deserve. I can't even keep myself on the right path. If it wasn't for the Holy Spirit working in my life, I'd be throwed off, too."

"Alright, preacher," JG said, throwing up his hands in surrender. "I get it. But you know what I mean."

"Yeah," Boss replied with a smile. "Lord knows that wife of mine is not going. She gon tell it like it is. And I need that."

As they were rounding the final stretch of the track for the third time, they saw the officer opening the gate. Yard time was just about over. This was good… for both of them.

"When was the last time you talked to Marcus?" Boss asked.

"Man, about two or three weeks ago. Every time I call, he's either too busy to talk or it just rings. I'll catch him eventually."

"Yeah, lil bruh hard at it. It was a lot more difficult than any of us could have expected. But he has the right help, and progress is being made in the right direction."

"You must've talked to him recently?"

"Yeah. I think it was last Thursday, maybe Friday. I was on the phone with Ebony when she stopped by the building they got. It's an old elementary school out east. It's a nice spot. It needs a lot of work before they can open, but they got a good price on it. Anyway, he hopped on the phone for a few minutes. He sounded exhausted! I think he was happy to be on the phone with me just so he could catch his breath." They both laughed.

"For real. He must be helping with the renovations?"

"Of course. When you're starting a business, even a non-profit, anything you can do to cut costs helps, so those Carpentry and Electrical Wiring Certificates he was so proud of are actually paying off. And those custodial skills he picked up when he was a rock man."

"Man, no wonder that fool so tired; he got ten jobs!"

"More than that. And he ain't getting paid for none of it. But he's straight. He'll reap his rewards in due time."

They finally started filing through the gate leaving the yard.

"I wonder if he's heard from Lil D?" JG pondered

"Ah, yeah. I knew I was forgetting something," Boss announced. "Lil D came down for the weekend last week. Even helped out as much as he could."

"That's what's up, man." JG said. "That's my dude."

"I thought you would've known that. You haven't talked to him either?"

"Nah, it's been about two weeks. He's busy too. I get annoyed when I call a certain amount of times and nobody answers. So, I just don't call for a while."

"Yeah, I used to be like that, but Ebony made me get over it," he said, shaking his head and laughing.

"How?"

"Like I told you, lil bruh; she don't play," he flatly stated as they walked into the front door of the unit.

That weekend JG received a surprise visit from Jessica. She had not made the trip since J Jr.'s birthday eight months ago. And to his astonishment, today she was alone. Since she had a boyfriend, she had made it clear that any visits would be for their son's sake. He understood, and that understanding made their relationship better. Without expectations, there were no letdowns. They no longer argued over trivial matters. She even helped with his business planning when she could. Things were great. So why was she up here, alone?

"Hey," she said, giving him a quick hug and sitting down.

"Hey," he responded suspiciously, "what's going on? Is everything alright?"

"Yeah. I just decided to ride up here and see how you were you doing?" she said, still trying to play it cool.

"Okay," JG answered, nodding his head. He sat back and threw his arms over the backs of the seats on either side of him. He cocked his head to the side and gave her a look over.

"What?" she asked, feigning innocence

"Ain't nothing. I'm just checking you out. I ain't seen you in awhile. You look good."

"Thank you," she replied, averting her eyes.

JG acted like he was clearing his throat as he stood up, stretched his arms out to the side, and turned around as if he were modeling.

Jessica cracked up. "My bad. You look good too."

"*Thank* you! I been killing myself working out. I know Tina told you about 'the beast!'"

"Nah," she answered, shaking her head and smiling, "she didn't tell me about 'the beast.'"

"She a hater! But I know you see it!"

"I guess so," she said, glad she came.

They spent the next couple of hours genuinely enjoying each other's presence. It had been a long time since they'd been alone. That is, as alone as you could be in a prison visitation gallery. Still, it left the both of them feeling nostalgic. When the visit was about to end, JG leaned over and tried to kiss her. She turned away and put her head down.

"What's up, Jessica?" he asked, confused.

She took a deep breath, lifted her head, and looked at him with what was unmistakably love.

"Jeremy, I've always loved you, and you know that. I had hoped to be over you before you got out. I believe I was on my way. To be honest you were making it easy for me." She let out a nervous laugh, and he could do nothing but nod his head in agreement with a smile on his face. "But over the last year or so you've changed. And I like it. But..."

"But, what?" he cut in.

She let out a deep sigh. "Let's just give it some time," she pleaded.

JG knew what it was. She didn't want to get hurt again. For all she knew, the moment he walked out of this place he would go right back to his old ways. She was right to protect herself. And she was also right about him. He had changed. A big part of that change was realizing how stupid he had been as far as she was concerned. He loved her, and he was willing to do whatever it took to earn her trust.

"Okay. I'm with it," he declared.

"Yeah?" she answered, relieved.

"Yeah," he said, smiling and blowing her a kiss.

✝

A couple of days later JG called to check on Lil D, who was appreciative but not yet willing to let the slight of him not calling go unnoticed.

"What's up, fool?!" JG exclaimed.

"What's up with you, man? Why you ain't been hitting me up?"

"Ah, man ... you know how it is. I know you be busy, and I don't feel like getting on your nerves by constantly calling."

"Man, cut it out! You didn't care about getting on my nerves when I was in the unit with you. Don't change up now!"

"Fool, if anything, it was you getting on my nerves," he joked.

"Yeahhh, you got me right there," Lil D conceded with a chuckle of his own. "So, what's up, man? How are things going?"

"Everything is good, homie. Ready to get out there and get at it."

"I already know. You still going to stay with your auntie?"

"Yeah. I think that's my best bet. It'll give me some time to get everything together without all the pressure of *having* to get it together. You feel me?"

"That's real, bruh. It was a struggle for me and my pops had me set up when I got out. A different sort of struggle, but a struggle nonetheless."

"I feel you," JG agreed. "Guess what, fool?"

"What's up?"

"Jessica came up here to see me by herself Saturday."

"Oh yeah!" Lil D exclaimed, happy for his friend. He knew how good she was for JG. "So ... is she coming back home?"

"Yeaaahhh?"

"What you mean, 'yeaaahhh'? She either is or she isn't."

"It ain't that simple, bruh. I scarred that girl. Unfaithful, disrespectful, the whole nine yards. You already know. I was awful homie. And she don't wanna get hurt again. She doesn't deserve to. So, she wanna just see how things play out once I touch down. I can't do nothing but respect that."

"Bruh, don't mess it up!" Lil D forcefully said.

"Man, who you posed to be? The Love Enforcer?"

Lil D laughed. "Nah, man. But remember who you came crying to when she started hanging up on you for shooting that ole tired game at her."

"Crying! Nah, you ain't never heard me crying. And ain't nothing tired about my game!" JG defiantly proclaimed.

"Hey, man," Lil D replied with a serious tone, "don't play yourself. You bet not let that pride rob you of something that good."

"Alright, fool. I got you," JG responded, softening his demeanor. "What you been up to?"

"The business, man. Everything we talked about, bruh. Like I told you, my pops had me set up. I'm just working on establishing myself right now."

"That's what's up, homie. How your fam doing?"

"Man, they're straight. Mama got us back on the Sunday family dinners. She doesn't allow no phones or nothing during that time. It ain't that much of a problem for me because I went a few years in there without all that. Plus, that thing can be a nuisance. My sister hates it though!" he said, laughing. "She calls herself being in love. So, when she can't be there to answer his call or text or whatever else they do to stay in touch, it kills her. Mama told her to invite him over, but they been making excuses why he can't make it. Probably can't get his nerves up to come and face the man of the house." He pompously declared.

"Man of the house, huh? I hear you. You getting everybody's love life in order, but I ain't heard a word about yours. You must still be taking those 'comprehensive' showers you loved so much in here?"

Lil D burst out laughing, "Man, you stupid!"

"You ain't denied it. I must be right."

"Nah, man. I got a gal. She actually came over Sunday. But I don't think my mama likes her."

"Why you think that?"

"I know my mama. It's cool though. She gon have to get over it. *I* like her."

"That's right. *You're* the man of the house."

"Whatever, man. Anyway, make sure you call Marcus. He said you been acting funny with him too."

"Yeah. Boss told me I needed to get over it."

"Really? So, when are you going to start listening?"

"I'm working on it, homie. I'm working on it."

CHAPTER 18

Boss was in the cell laying on the bunk reading Dondre Whitfield's *Male vs. Man* when the pod officer knocked on the door and informed him that he had an attorney visit. His lawyer hadn't said anything about coming to see him, so he was caught off guard.

"Okay. Give me a few minutes."

The visit was totally unexpected, so it took him a while to get dressed and ready to go. He didn't know what the occasion was, but it had to be pretty important, good or bad, for him to just pop up like this.

Walking out of the front door of the unit he took a deep breath, inhaling the ambiance of mid-winter in the mountains. The air was cold, thin, and clean. The prison farm had several cows, which produced the milk consumed at the institution. And the odors they gave off would have been unbearable if it wasn't for the smell of burning applewood coming from the chimney of the warden's quarters on the hill overlooking the prison grounds.

Boss was by no means a country boy. In fact, most of his upbringing had taken place in the bricks of one housing project or another. However, as a young boy he had found great pleasure in spending the occasional summer on his grandparents' farm. And if he ever made it out, he planned on trading in his Jordan's for a pair of Tecovas.

Making it to the visitation gallery, he was searched by an officer and escorted to a small conference room where his attorney was waiting. Mr. Pressi stood up to shake his hand and they sat down at the table across from one another.

"So, what's going on, Scott? It must be important for you to drive all this way without letting me know you were coming."

"It is," he said, passing Boss a manila envelope. "I got this yesterday."

"Yesterday!" Boss replied, even more surprised. "What is it?"

"It's an order from the Sixth Circuit," he answered, looking directly at Boss, his face giving nothing away.

"So, what did they say, man?" he said, getting a little agitated with apprehension.

"Well ... nothing is final, of course. We still have a fight ahead of us, but..." he stopped short, smiling, unable to disguise his emotion.

"But... what?" Boss demanded with growing anticipation.

"They ruled in our favor, Otis."

"What?" Boss couldn't believe it. "So..." was all he managed to get out before being rendered speechless. He had been fighting for so long. He had endured so many defeats and setbacks that at times he had wanted to give up. It often seemed like the appeals process was simply another apparatus created by the "system" to slowly crush the hopes of the incarcerated and their families. Now he was being told that through this unjust, uncaring, unscrupulous process, he had been granted a victory. And not just any victory, but one that would resonate throughout the prison system, impacting thousands who were unjustifiably prosecuted. A most improbable victory. In fact, it was too good to be true. So, although he wanted to be, almost needed to be, excited about this, he wouldn't allow it. He was well aware of how this process worked. *The courts giveth, and the courts taketh away*, he thought.

"So where are we at?" he asked, all business.

"Well, you know as well as I do how this goes. They will appeal, of course. They have to. A ruling like this has huge ramifications. This could be a watershed moment in the history of criminal justice reform. Just think about what this would mean retroactively," he observed, aware of the fight ahead. "But Otis," he said, looking at him with a fierceness in his eyes, "I really believe we've got em this time."

Boss stared across the table at Sam Pressi. It was rare to find an attorney who was as passionate about your case as you were. Most of them were strictly in it for the paycheck. Any zeal they displayed in pursuing victory was to uphold their reputation and to maintain a steady stream of income. Sam was different. Although his representation was not cheap, the money was not the primary motivation. He believed in the Constitution; therefore, he fought tooth and nail to preserve the rights written therein. If he believed you to be guilty and rightfully prosecuted, he would not touch your case. However, if you've been wronged in any way contrary to the U.S. constitution, once you hired him your cause become his in a manner that even close family finds difficult to acquire.

"Thank you, Sam," he said, nodding his head to express his gratitude.

"For what? This is what you paid me for. I'm just doing my job," he replied with a sly smile, closing his briefcase and standing up.

"Yeah, well I wish everyone did their job with as much integrity as you."

"Well ... let's just hope the Supreme Court shows that same integrity when they make their ruling."

"Amen," Boss agreed, shaking his head before they parted ways.

He walked back to the unit in a daze. What he and so many others had been fervently praying for had apparently come to pass, yet he found it hard to believe. It was like the account in the Book of Acts when the church was praying for Peter's deliverance from prison and death, but when the Lord brought it about, they questioned whether it was real or not.

Normally he would have called Ebony as soon as he received such amazing news, but not today. Instead, he went to his cell, put a William Murphy CD in the radio, and lay there twenty minutes until he decided to finally read the order for himself. Maybe he would find something to temper his expectations. Yet, the more he read, the more he realized why his attorney was so optimistic. *We got em*, he thought, against his better judgement. He read it once more, laid it back on the desk, and drifted off to sleep listening to, "Everything Is Working for My Good."

✝

Later on that night, he finally called Ebony. He had been anxious about telling her the news all day. Of everyone, including himself, she had been most expectant that some way, somehow, he would be given another chance. Her faith in God's ability and willingness to "abundantly pardon" and turn hearts in his favor had never wavered.

"What's up, baby?" she jovially asked when she answered the phone.

"Hey!" he replied, smiling "Somebody's in a good mood."

"I sure am!" she excitedly affirmed. "Baby, God is really good."

"All the time," he agreed, wondering if she already knew. "So, what's going on," he inquired?

"Well, you know how much trouble I was having with Tae."

"Yeah."

"Well, recently we've been spending more personal time together. Taking our lunch breaks together and sitting around the shop for a little while after we close up enjoying some girl talk. She even comes over on the occasional weekend just to be around me. Which Vanessa can't stand, but that's another story," she said, rolling her eyes as if Boss could see her. "Anyway, after work today, I was taking her home and we had a real heart to heart. She shared some things with me that had been burdening her for a long time. And Otis," she paused, putting emphasis on her words, "she's hurting. She needs our help, and our prayers."

She was crying now. Whatever it was Tae had revealed to her was painful, and Ebony has made a choice to bear the burden as if it were her own. And Boss would be there to shoulder as much as was needed.

"I'm sorry to hear that, baby."

"No, Otis. There's nothing to be sorry about. As bad as it is, this is what it took to get her where she is," she replied, smiling through her tears. "See, as we were talking and crying, I had to pull the car over because the Spirit was moving so strongly. And right there, in a Krystal's parking lot, Tae surrendered her life, with all her hurts and pains, to the Lordship of Jesus Christ."

"Hallelujah!" Boss exclaimed, still amazed at how often God does the unexpected.

"So yes," Ebony concluded, "I'm in a *great* mood today."

"Amen. Well, I've had a pretty good day myself."

"Really? What happened?"

"Scott came to see me today."

"And?"

"And we got em."

"What?" Her voice softened again, and he heard a faint whimper emanating from her. "Are you serious baby?" she cried, muttering praise to the One she clearly attributed all blessings to.

"Yeah, baby, I'm serious. They actually ruled that the feds violated the Double Jeopardy Clause when they prosecuted me after the state already had."

"But I thought ..." she began, at a loss for words.

"I know, baby," he continued, as amazed as she was. "It's hard for me to believe. This was the definition of a long shot. They've been violating and upholding the Fifth Amendment for ages using the separate-sovereigns doctrine. There are so many men and women in this country serving state and federal sentence for the exact same offenses that it's ridiculous. But thanks to the Gamble case in 2019, and especially the dissenting opinions, we decided to go for it. And if the Supreme Court upholds this ruling, thousands of others and I will get the justice we deserve. And future generations of Americans won't be subjected to more time than their crimes warrant. It's not just a win for us. It's a win for justice," he proudly stated.

"That's incredible, Otis." she said, tears slowly streaming down her face. And it was. Anyone who had any experience with the appellate process knew how arbitrary it was. You could have two separate cases, with the same elements and circumstances, arguing the same issues. Yet a judge in the Second Circuit and another judge in the Tenth Circuit could make totally different rulings, and both be right. In the issue Boss had raised concerning Double Jeopardy, most judges never actually ruled based on the merits of the case. They simply stated that, "For 170 years the courts have always recognized the separate-sovereigns doctrine," so they would as well. It's the equivalent of saying that, though slavery is wrong, because it has always existed in America, we agree that it should continue to exist. Think about where this country would be if that was the prevailing reasoning of our judiciary.

CHAPTER 19

Boss had done his best to keep the news from coming out, and not because he didn't want others to know. On the contrary, he looked forward to the day when prisoners and their families nationwide received this jolt of hope. He just didn't want it to happen prematurely, and possibly only temporarily. Because he knew how the courts operated, he chose to keep it under wraps. Yet, unbeknownst to him, and despite his efforts, there were beginning to be whispers about the ruling.

He was sitting on a crate and pillow next to his cell door reading the latest issue of *The Sun* when JG walked up on him.

"Big bruh," he said excitedly, almost knocking the magazine out of Boss' hand with a slap on the shoulder. "Man, why didn't you come holler at me? I heard about the good news!"

"What news?" he asked, genuinely confused, wondering if he had betrayed his own intentions.

"Come on, Bossman. You know what I'm talking about. You bout to get up out of here!"

"Who told you that?" he suspiciously asked.

"I talked to Marcus last night. He said he called Ebony a few days ago and she was crying. He asked if she was alright, and she told him about your case being overturned. He got so emotional about it that he started crying too. He always was kind of sensitive," JG commented, always the jokester. "That's what's up, man. I'm happy for you, big bruh."

"Yeah, but you know how these things can go. The judge ruled in my favor; they appealed. The next judge might rule in their favor. Then I'll appeal. It goes on and on. So, don't get too excited. Not yet."

"I feel you, big bruh. I do. But I've been around you for a while now. I see you pouring your life into the dudes in here. Into me! You bring light to this place. Especially this unit. It wouldn't be the same without you. For real," JG said, nodding his head.

"And before you say it," he continued, with a knowing smile on his face, "I know it's only by the grace of God. But from what I know about God, you had to let Him use you. He didn't force you to. You chose to. Now, He is about to use you out there, where it's really needed. I may not believe like you do, but I truly believe that. And I don't know *anybody* who deserves it more. So, you can play it cool, but I'm excited for you, big bruh."

Even if he wanted to say something in response, he couldn't find the words. Because in his inner man, he believed it. Not so much that he was deserving of it, but that it was part of God's purpose for his life. The Lord had made him "ruler" over a few things, and now he was going to entrust him with a bigger ministry, a greater influence, a more global impact. So instead of attempting to strengthen his own point, he simply conceded with a heartfelt, "Amen," and let it be.

As agreed upon, JG and Jessica were taking it slow, which turned out to be the start of something special. When he was out, JG never actually took the time to get to know any of the women he fooled around with. Which made it easier for him, because there were never any real feelings involved. As long as he kept it on a strictly carnal level, he never had to worry about feeling bad about the way he treated them. Plus, it made it easier to just dismiss them.

But now that he was getting to know Jessica, and opening himself up to being known by her, he was beginning to enjoy her in a way that was both exciting and scary. Although he liked it, processing it was still difficult for someone who had never experienced it. He had always known that she loved him, but the thought of genuinely loving any woman who wasn't family was foreign to him. He needed some counsel. He normally would've turned to Boss, but he wanted a different perspective.

Leaving the cell, he walked downstairs and jumped on the phone. After three rings a woman answered and accepted the collect call.

"Hello?" he inquired, with a curious smile on his face.

Lil D had been out almost two years now. He'd met Jennifer, whose little sister had nicknamed her GiGi when they were children, about nine months ago. They had both attended an event for small business owners. She was a personal trainer who operated out of a small studio gym not too far from Lil D's detail shop. By coincidence, or fate, they had arrived at the same time, parking next to one another. They noticed an attraction from the start, but neither initially acted upon it. Yet they kept "bumping into" one another throughout the day. At breaks, they just happened to be at the same coffee machine. There were several food truck vendors parked outside for the hour lunch break; again, they ended up going to the same one. GiGi's recollection is that he was slick stalking her. Lil D attests that he was just in the mood for a "Sizzlin Salad." JG knew which story made sense to him. In all the time they were locked up together, he had never seen Lil D in the mood for a salad of any kind.

Whatever the case, by the end of the day they left the parking lot having exchanged numbers and coming to the conclusion that they enjoyed spending time with one another. Over time it became more of a need, and now she was in his apartment answering his phone.

"Hey, Jeremy. How are you doing?"

"Considering the circumstances, I'm pretty good, GiGi. You must be good, too. I see my guy ain't ran you off yet," he joked.

"Nahhh. He tries but I'm not going anywhere. He wouldn't know what to do without me," she quipped in return.

"You're on speaker, man! I can hear y'all," Lil D yelled from the kitchen counter, where he was finishing off a slice of cheesecake.

"We weren't whispering homie. We wanted you to hear us," JG shot back.

GiGi laughed and took her fiancé the phone. She appreciated the bond he and JG had. "Bye, Jeremy," she said before walking off into the back of the house.

Lil D wiped his mouth with a napkin and picked up the phone. "What's going on, man?"

"Not too much, man. Trying to stay focused. It's almost over with."

"Yeah, I know. Have you decided where you're going when you get out?"

"Oh, I'm still going to my Aunt Trish's. That's locked in," he said in a resolute manner.

"I know that's been your plan for a while now. I just figured you were considering going all in with Jessica the way things are going."

He chuckled and said, "Homie, I'm in further than I thought possible already."

"Uh-oh," Lil D expressed with a knowing tone.

"Yeah, man," JG almost grunted in response. "She got me. I mean... like... *got* me! But it ain't that bad, man," he grudgingly admitted.

"So why are you making it sound like a problem that needs to be solved?"

"Because it is! I don't know what I'm doing, homie! I ain't never loved no gal like this."

"Mannn, don't none of us know what we're doing! We weren't schooled in this. My parents were married almost forty years, but my father never sat me down and talked to me about how to maintain a relationship with a woman. And he saw me stumbling into and out of one bad relationship after another. He was a great man in many ways, but he failed in that area. Like most fathers."

"Yeah," JG agreed.

"But it's alright, man," Lil D continued. "I'm finding out that's the real beauty of it. Figuring it out. Together."

"And what are you figuring out?" JG asked, seriously. He needed to know.

"You joked that I hadn't run GiGi off yet. But believe me, if she wasn't committed to *us,* she could find a reason to get on down. So could I. She's amazing, and I am blessed to have her. But she's no more perfect than I am. We're just devoted to loving one another. Good or bad."

"Man, you've really grown up, homie."

"I've been trying to tell you since I got out that I was the man of the family," Lil D jabbed at him.

"Oh, yeah. I forgot. My bad, homie."

"But seriously man," Lil D advised, "just embrace it."

"Listen to him, Jeremy," GiGi hollered in the background.

"Man, you still got me on speaker!" JG exclaimed.

"Of course not. But she's right here. She didn't need to hear you to know what we're talking about."

"Yeah, I guess not," he said. Then, almost wondering out loud, "Is this what I'm gon have to put up with? Jessica knowing all my business?"

"Yes, Jeremy, you are," GiGi answered, as she was now holding the phone. "And you'll learn to love it."

JG heard laughter and a rustling noise in the phone as Lil D wrestled the phone out of her hands. When he spoke into the phone, he sounded a little winded, and very happy.

"Welcome to the other side, man. I gotta go. I got some business to handle. Love you, bruh." And he hung up.

CHAPTER 20

Boss and JG walked toward intake side by side, a small net bag containing photos and legal envelopes slung over JG's shoulder. He was about to walk out of prison, and be reunited with his son, Jessica, Aunt Trish, and Tina. It was indeed a time of celebration. Boss seemed to be as excited for him as he was for himself.

Still, leaving Boss behind was difficult. He was the last of "the crew." He had met many men through this prison experience, but a few had actually become family. Silence (R.I.P), Lil D, and Marcus had been released. Now he, like the others, would be leaving Boss in this place, not knowing when, or if, he would be joining them on the outside. It was bittersweet, and he was having a hard time expressing what he felt. Boss, being Boss, understood his position and did his best to ease his uneasiness.

"Look, lil bruh, don't let *nothing* dampen this for you. On the other side of that door you're getting ready to walk through is the life you've been preparing for. There are some very special and important people waiting on you, and you should be overjoyed. You don't have to feel guilty about it. Not for my sake."

"I know man, but...."

"No buts! This is your day. Embrace it; enjoy it! I've done this more than a few times, lil bruh. I am genuinely happy for you. This makes every investment worth it. Seeing you go out there and be the father, husband, nephew, cousin, friend, entrepreneur, and *son* God has called you to be."

That last one was hard for JG to swallow, but he knew Boss was right. He had missed the majority of his son's young life, even before he was sent to prison. He hoped he'd be forgiven, and he needed to do the same. He had no intention of inviting either his father, who was still in federal prison, or his mother into his everyday life. But he would honor them with the respect their title deserved and help out if they needed him, when he could.

"I got you, Bossman. I appreciate you not giving up on me as a lost cause."

"Come on, man. You know I don't believe in lost causes. If Jesus can save and transform someone as messed up as me, ain't nothing He can't do."

"You gon preach to me all the way to the gate, ain't you?" JG poked at him.

"I'll walk through the gate *with you* preaching if they let me," Boss replied, both men laughing.

"Your day is coming, big bruh," JG attested, stopping at the gate you have to go through in order to get to intake.

Boss just nodded his head, neither affirming nor denying the statement. He was content with whatever the Lord's will was for his life.

"Come here, man," he said, giving JG a hug that only someone who has been in the "trenches" of life with another can understand.

"I love you, big bruh!" JG exclaimed, pressing the button that alerted the guard stationed in the control booth that he was ready to go.

"I love you, too, lil bruh."

Boss watched him walk through the intake door and took off back toward the unit. He had indeed done this more than a few times. He was genuinely happy and excited every time for those men. Yet, that didn't make it any easier on him. *I would love to finally be the one on the other side of this exchange,* he thought. Or maybe it was a prayer. Lord knows he meant it.

✝

A few days later Boss called to check on Marcus. Things hadn't exactly gone as expected since he'd been out. As prepared as he was, there are some things you just don't plan for. Others you couldn't plan for if you tried. It just so happened that one of the organizations he was partnering with had some shady business practices going on. They were being investigated for fraud, and since they had invested a substantial amount into Redeeming the Silence, progress had come to a halt until the investigation concluded. It was a blow to Marcus, but also a learning experience. Although he wasn't responsible for bringing them into the fold, he was going to make sure he vetted every potential network moving forward. He wasn't going to allow someone else's actions or reputation tear down what he was building.

He didn't answer the first time Boss called, so he hit right back. Marcus picked up on the first ring this time and quickly accepted the call.

"What's up, big bruh? Man, I'm glad you called back."

"Yeah, I know this crooked phone system is jacked up a lot, so I always try to hit back just to be sure. So how are you?"

"Ah, I'm good, big bruh. I lost my focus a lil bit after everything went down the way it did. But I remembered some of the lessons I learned in there about how to respond when your life is negatively impacted by things that are out of your control. So, I went into 'lockdown mode' and regrouped."

"Oh yeah," Boss said, smiling. It was always refreshing to talk to one of the few who actually took those life lessons with them. Society has the misconception that life somehow stops when you're incarcerated. But nothing could be further from the truth. Some may make the unfortunate choice to stop living. But for the few who choose to live, despite their circumstances, prison can be a life transforming experience. Males become men.

"So, what did you come up with?" Boss inquired.

"Well, I'm going to school."

"Finally!" Boss exclaimed.

Marcus grinned. "Yeah, I figured that's how you'd respond."

"It's the right move, lil bruh."

"I agree," he conceded. "This investigation was like a blessing in disguise. You know I've always wanted to go to college. When I first got locked up, I lost my enthusiasm. By the time I started to get it back, I was focused on other things. When I first got out, Redeeming the Silence consumed all of my time. But now..."

"I *get* it, man. I'm happy for you. And it'll only help when things do get back rolling."

"Exactly," Marcus agreed.

"So how is everything else going?"

"Everything is good, big bruh. I really needed this break from the 'busyness' of it all. I went and spent a weekend with my family last week. I didn't realize how long it had been and how much I needed it. We needed it."

"That's good, man," Boss interjected.

"Yeah, big bruh," Marcus continued, "it was. I took my little sister to the mall, went fishing with my mama, and played some Scrabble with my dad. And we all went to church Sunday. The whole weekend was a blessing. I made a commitment to myself to get up there at least one weekend every month no matter what. As long as I'm physically able, I'm going."

"Amen."

"I ran into an old friend, too," he craftily tossed in.

"Okay," Boss responded, interest piqued. "What kind of 'old friend' are we talking about."

"A girl who I grew up around. She lived a few houses down the street from me. She's like six years older than I am. I had a big crush on her and she knew it, but she wasn't going. She had moved away before I `came of age` so to speak. I hadn't seen her since. But while I was locked up, she had moved back home. She saw me in my parents' driveway and came over to speak. We ended up spending an hour or so sitting on the porch catching up. She seemed to be impressed. And I can't lie, I was too."

"Okay then," Boss said smiling. "You better be careful, though. Don't get caught up in your teenage fantasy."

Marcus started laughing. "Big bruh, no joke, when we first started talking some of those old images ran through my mind. It probably ran through hers too." The thought of that made him laugh again, remembering how he used to follow her around and how she would tease him by calling him "my lil boyfriend."

"Yeah," he carried on, "that was a trip. But the longer we talked, all of that was history. She was a woman, and I was a man, and we obviously liked one another."

"So, what does she do?"

"She's a school teacher."

"Oh, so she's another lil boy's teenage fantasy?"

Marcus hadn't considered that. "Now that you mention it, she probably has a classroom full of lil horny Marcuses." They both laughed.

"So, what's going on with you, bruh?" Marcus asked.

"Trying to stay focused, lil bruh."

"Yeah."

"You know, at no time since I've been down have I ever given up on walking out of here. I trusted God and did all I could as far as filing appeals and what not. All the while I was laser focused on the ministry and my purpose in being here.

"And it's not like I've abandoned that. But there are times when I know I'm not focused because I am thinking about the reality of getting out of here now. It's not just theory any longer. You understand what I'm saying?"

"Absolutely. And I don't think you should feel bad about it, if that's what's going on."

"I've been gone a long time lil bruh. So, trust me, I definitely don't feel bad about the prospect of walking up out of here in the near future." Boss clarified. "I just don't wanna allow myself to become so focused on tomorrow that I miss today. Jesus might come back before tomorrow gets here."

"I feel you, big bruh. But I know you. I've witnessed your commitment to God's purpose for your life."

"Yeah, but I'm only human. And any human who has been locked away for this long, separated from wife, kids, and everything else dear to you would be somewhat distracted. Even anxious. And not just for myself. I'm anxious for anybody who didn't give up on me. For everybody in here who has given up on their situation. I want them to see the glory of God through this."

"They will big bruh. I know it," Marcus assured him. He wanted to see it too. "So have you heard anything else?"

"Not officially. But," he said suspiciously, "Sam, my attorney, is coming to see me Thursday. I didn't get to talk to him. I spoke to his secretary, so I don't know why. It definitely means something but..."

"It's your time, big bruh," Marcus stated, excited for this man he met in prison at the lowest point in his life, who had become family.

"We'll see, man. To God be the glory."

"Amen," Marcus concluded, sounding a lot like Boss.

"Amen," Boss echoed.

"Oh yeah. So, I've had a lot of extra time on my hands, and I started back writing. I haven't done it in a while, but I want you to check this out before we get off the phone."

"Okay. That's what's up. Let me hear it."

"Alright." Marcus said, clearing his throat before taking off:

"There's nothing quite like family.
I'm talking about those who crouch down
in the trenches with you.
And never consider a Plan B.
I mean, the ones who express their love with action.
The kind that never loses its grip;
Instead, as it travels along the road it only gains
traction.
The love I'm speaking of never budges.
It instinctively rises above holding onto grudges, and
the judgment.
They share more with you than DNA.
This bond goes deeper than blood, where you're from,
and a last name.
The family I refer to was acquired with the currency
of challenging circumstances.
When I thought I wouldn't make it unless I had
another to stand with.
Love that withstood the times of inconvenience,
Or worse;
When tragedy struck, and I couldn't flee it
I pay homage to those who absorbed my tears.
Those who helped me to fight through the insecurities
and calmed my fears.
You are my family, and I salute you.
You weren't simply born into it, and I didn't have to
recruit you.
You made a definitive choice of me.
And today I use my voice to triumphantly,
Proclaim before heaven and earth that I am eternally
grateful.

> *When the Lord blessed me with you*
> *He gave me a plate full.*
> *My cup...runneth... over."*

Boss was speechless. The words of this poem pierced his heart. His foolish choices had deprived him of the family he was born into. The Lord had given him a new one. He too was grateful.

"So, what do you think, big bruh?" Marcus inquired, put off by the silence.

Taking another moment to reflect, Boss responded in typical fashion. "Amen."